DO NOT REMOVE
CARDS FROM POCKET

DEATH
ON THE
BROADLANDS

DEATH ON THE BROADLANDS

ALAN HUNTER

Walker and Company
New York

Death on the Broadlands
was originally published in England
as *Amorous Leander.*

Copyright © 1983 Alan Hunter

First published in the United States of America
in 1984 by the Walker Publishing Company, Inc.

Published simultaneously in Canada by John Wiley & Sons
Canada, Limited, Rexdale, Ontario.

Library of Congress Cataloging in Publication Data

Hunter, Alan.
  Death on the broadlands.

  I. Title.
PR6015.U565D39 1984   823'.914   83-40430
ISBN 0-8027-5590-9

Printed in the United States of America

10 9 8 7 6 5 4 3 2 1

7136588

'This is Keith, my dear. He's my nephew from Cambridge. I believe he is studying physics when he isn't writing verse. Unless you like sonnets to your eyebrow, you would do well not to encourage him.'

Stella came out of the reverie she had fallen into over her sherry and, shaping her lips into a smile, gave the young man her hand. She didn't particularly notice him since she had given up paying attention to men. But she managed the smile, and a complimentary flick of her eyelashes.

'He's my brother Iain's son. Notice the undistinguished chin.'

'Yes. Like yours.'

'It's the stamp of the Lea-Stephens.'

The young man flushed and scuffed one of his sandals against the other. Then he said, blurting it out:

'I've read your last book, Miss Rushton.'

'It was probably my worst.'

'Oh no, I didn't think so.'

Simon laughed. He punched his tall nephew on the shoulder. 'You'll learn, my son, that a writer's last book is always his worst. But now you'd better run along – we're having supper in ten minutes. You look as though you had just come back from a safari.'

The approach of supper was confirmed by a rattle of cutlery in the next room and Ruby, Simon's maid, had just been in to receive instructions. Casually, without real intention, Stella had watched Simon talking to her, at the same time thinking how irreproachably he filled the role of a successful man. He had confidence and poise and just the right manner for everyone. His voice, clear and resonant, barely hinted at a costly schooling. Though he was short his figure was neat and he had unfairly photogenic features: smiling grey eyes under straight, dark brows, a straight nose and a handsome forehead. He was the illustrated weeklies' idea of a best-selling writer and had often been photographed in this very room in his 'idyllic Broadland retreat'. As he came back to her now he made his smile personal, for Stella.

'I shouldn't ask you, I know, but are you working on something new?'

'Yes. A new novel.'

'I wondered if you'd taken the cottage for a rest.'

'I have in a way.'

'But work is the best antidote?'

She shrugged feebly, keeping her eyes fixed on her glass. He knew, the world knew, why she was burying herself down here.

'I'd sooner not talk about it.'

'I'm damned clumsy, I know. But I thought I would like to say a word before the others came in. I hate to think of you alone there.'

'It's what I want more than anything.'

'I know you do, Stella dear. But is that entirely wise?'

Staring at the glass, she was very much afraid that she was going to burst into tears; she saw it grow larger and mistier and its outlines become confused. It was perhaps her resentment that saved her; she resented his tone of superior wisdom. He wanted to be kind, she appreciated that, but how could he begin to understand her situation?

'I really would rather not talk about it.'

'Forgive me, my dear. I felt I had to bring it up.'

'It's – it's too personal a matter.'

'Yes, I see it is, now. I really am the biggest fool, you know. I think I can rush in anywhere and sort out things for whoever.'

He turned away abruptly and went across to the cabinet to pour himself another drink. From the direction of the French windows, down the terrace and across the lawn, came the sound of an outboard motor kicking itself to a halt. Simon's guests had arrived back from an evening spin on the Broad.

6

'You seem so solitary, my dear . . . one feels obliged to do what one can.' Simon returned to her slowly, his grey eyes lowered earnestly.

'It's kind of you, Simon. But the cottage is all I want.'

'At the same time –' he touched glasses with her – 'do remember that we're here. You needn't starve yourself of company with Lazy Waters around the corner. You'll soon get to know the folks, and Keith – you've met him already. So treat us like friends. Drop in whenever you have the mind.'

'Thank you, Simon.'

She could feel herself on the point of tears again, but voices were approaching, and, biting her lip, she stood up. Simon gently squeezed her hand and gave her a look of encouragement. Then the French windows swung open and the others came in.

2

It was barely a month since Stella Rushton's world had tumbled about her ears, and only a fortnight since she had first become acquainted with Simon. She had met him before – their paths had crossed at a publisher's reception – but then she had paid him little attention, and certainly he had paid her none. The occasion had been the launch of his current book. She had formed part of the toasting, admiring fringe. They had shaken hands, and smiled, and then he had promptly forgotten her; and she, just then living in a blissful paradise, had been content to be forgotten. The reception had been in January. Now it was the beginning of July. During that interval Simon's book had made a fortune, while Stella had wanted to give up living.

Yet it had been such a commonplace affair, the sort that happens every day of the year; for there is always a foolish woman somewhere ready to throw her heart at a man. This man's name was Justin Hamilton and unfortunately he was very well-known. He was an ex-yachtsman who had broken numerous records for sailing round the world single-handed. But he was also well-known because of his dead wife, the French helmswoman Françoise Durand, whom he had rescued in a daring exploit when she had been wrecked in the Coral Sea. There had been a quick, romantic wedding when the two of them had landed at Rockhampton, Queensland; but a year later Françoise had vanished while competing in the Fastnet race. And to Stella, a youngish novelist neither well-known nor much regarded, had fallen the job of writing the history of this interesting business.

She had been put on to it by her publisher, who was a relative of Hamilton's, and though the task didn't greatly appeal to her she couldn't afford to turn it down. She had driven out to Godalming, where Hamilton now lived. She had been easily persuaded to stay at his house with his smart but friendly sister. By profession Hamilton was a marine underwriter; he had a wide circle of friends, and into this circle Stella had slipped with a readiness that surprised her. And she had fallen in love with Justin, it was as simple, as natural as that. She was thirty-two, but it seemed like the first time it had ever happened to her.

He was a man to fall in love with. He was tall, broad-shouldered, and ruggedly handsome. He had questing blue eyes and an injured mouth and reddish-brown hair that curled crisply. He played golf and was the local tennis tiger and drove his pale green Mercedes with flair; at the office he wore beautifully tailored suits, but at home shaggy tweeds that smelled of tobacco. In addition, he was regarded by all his friends as a confirmed widower. His heart, yielded to the lost Françoise, had never been touched by another woman. He was gay to cover his sorrow and he jested to hide a tear; he was gallant, and romantic, and entirely irresistible.

And thus it was not very remarkable that Stella should fall in love with him, since during the writing of the book she had every opportunity. In his well-appointed study or under the cedar on his lawn they enjoyed a succession of tête-à-têtes as he related his experiences. He had a strangely caressing voice which she could listen to for hours. He answered, with never-failing patience, the questions she thought up to put to him. He taught her golf, admired her writing, and let her drive him in the Mercedes, and was her squire rather than his sister's when they went to visit friends. No, the truly remarkable thing – it seemed a miracle to Stella – was that Justin, without any urging, was apparently falling in love with her. She didn't rate her chances so high for she knew that her looks were not sensational, and there were prettier women of his acquaintance who must have baited their hooks for years.

But it happened. One day, in the autumn, when they had gone for a stroll in the beechwoods, he took her suddenly, clumsily in his arms and gave her a long, searching kiss. The strength had gone right out of her body; she had lain inert in the cradle of his arms. Drawing his head back and gazing down at her, he'd said:

'Little fool! You knew I wanted that.'

Later, with reckless greediness, she had told over each memory of those seconds, making certain that one by one they were impressed on her heart. She had recalled the exact scent of the falling damp leaves, the feel of the moss under her feet, the whimpering of Jock, his retriever. They had walked back out of the wood with their arms around each other, her face pressed against the warm tweed of his jacket; they had lingered at the gates watching the red westering sun, the smoke rising from cottage chimneys, the bands of frosty mist. It had all seemed new and incommunicably beautiful. She had wanted to cry because she had never before known such beauty.

She had been impossibly happy. She had scarcely noticed what happened round her. She went on working at the book but hardly knew what she was setting down. She never questioned the future, never gave or extracted a promise, never thought to be jealous or to make any claim on him. Indeed she had lived a dream, a dream she had thought without end; she loved and was beloved and asked no more from life than that. She welcomed each new day because it added to her happiness.

In the spring the book was finished and she knew the first moments of unease. Of course, until they were married she

9

couldn't continue living at Beechings. For one thing, Justin's sister was going abroad after Easter, and Justin had explained to her that, for professional reasons, he needed to be tender of his reputation. It was a wrench all the same to return to the neglected flat in Kensington. She made some half-hearted enquiries about accomodation in Godalming. Justin drove her up to town and they arranged to meet again two days later, but when the door closed behind him she couldn't help a flood of tears.

They met, they met again; nothing apparently had changed; in Justin's arms she buried the memories of the empty days without him. She introduced him to her friends and he seemed always charmed to meet them, he took her out to fashionable restaurants, the latest shows, the in-trend nightclubs. Her book, which had brought them together, continued to exert its benevolent influence; unlike her novels it seemed to be worth a great deal of expensive pre-publicity. There were receptions held in aid of it, she and Justin gave interviews. Pictures of them, usually together, were appearing frequently in the press. Their names were linked by gossip columnists. He didn't appear to resent this. Her friends made knowing remarks about them and these he accepted with a smile. In fact, except for those aching absences she was even happier than before, and the spring, an agreeably fine one, flew by on perfumed wings.

At the end of May Justin was obliged to attend some conference in Bermuda and she had known for some time in advance that she must lose him for a fortnight. She tried to be firm with herself about this – not to let him go for a fortnight was ridiculous! – but as the date of his departure drew near she became nervous and depressed. In the end she suggested she should go with him.

'I wouldn't be in the way, darling. I promise I wouldn't.'

His watchful blue eyes studied her face for a moment and then he replied:

'I'm sorry darling, but we must draw a line at that.'

'But Justin, why? I could take a later flight.'

'No.' He shook his head. 'Don't try to understand these

things. Besides, you'd be awfully bored. My time is all taken up. I've got to attend every session of this cursed conference, and in my spare time I'll have to write my reports.'

'But I'd see you every day –'

'Only at mealtimes, I'm afraid, and then it wouldn't be wise for you to stay at my hotel.'

She could understand his point but she couldn't help feeling hurt. It would have been more complimentary if for once he had sunk his caution. On the other hand, she secretly adored the manly firmness of his decision, and she resigned herself to staying in London because that was what Justin wanted of her. She saw him off at Heathrow. He looked uncompromisingly English. He wore a bowler and a black suit and a perfectly knotted RYS tie. He carried copies of *The Times* and *The Illustrated London News*, and just through the barrier he turned and touched his hat before disappearing. She took a taxi back to Kensington and settled down to weep.

Three days later, in the *Telegraph*, her eye fell on an announcement of his engagement. He was to marry the daughter of the chairman of a shipping line whose home was in Bermuda.

3

In the flat below hers lived a business girl, Jenny Williams, and if it hadn't been for Jenny, Stella didn't know what she would have done. On reading the announcement she had stupidly fainted and fallen heavily on the floor; it was Saturday, Jenny was at home, and the sound of the fall had brought her upstairs. When Stella came round she was lying on her settee. Jenny was sitting on a chair by her, swabbing her forehead with eau-de-Cologne. She had made a pot of tea of a strength that was truly formidable, and the *Telegraph* had disappeared, though there were some ashes in Stella's hearth.

'Now drink this, my dear – drink it quick, you understand?'

Jenny was Welsh and her soft voice was at once kindly and authoritative. She was the daughter, Stella knew, of a Nonconformist preacher, and she worked as a secretary in one of the publishing houses. Though they had been neighbours for several months Stella had never found her very approachable. Now Jenny sat stiffly, with a solemn face, while Stella sipped the mahogany tea.

'You gave me a fright, you did, my dear. You've been out cold for half an hour. I was going to call in the doctor, but then I saw you flutter your eyelids.'

'I'm sorry.'

'Oh, never mind that. Just drink your tea, and I'll pour you another.'

'I've just had . . . a shock.'

'Well drink your tea. You can talk about it after.'

Stella didn't want to talk about it. She dared scarcely even to think. She felt that when she faced it again she would be driven out of her mind. She wanted to lie in a dull stupor, her mind contracted into the space of the room; she wanted to fall into a sleep from which there would never be any waking. And sleep she did, because Jenny had slipped a sleeping-tablet into her cup. When she woke it was six o'clock and the table was being set for a meal.

That night the Welsh girl slept on Stella's settee and in the morning she fetched one or two of her things into the flat. She tended Stella like a child who was made fractious by some complaint, and unless she was sleeping, refused to let her alone for a moment. She talked brightly and persistently. Stella's only escape was into tears. Jenny's remedy for these was an immediate cup of tea, which was ruthlessly effective: one couldn't cry while drinking tea.

'You're cruel – cruel to me!'

'Now, my dear, you mustn't take on.'

'You don't understand. I'd rather die.'

'You wouldn't, my dear. You're not quite yourself.'

'At least, if I died –'

'I think I'll make a pot of tea.'

She slept that night quite exhausted, too tired even to cry. She hated Jenny with a fierce intensity though she knew that the Welsh girl was being a trump. She wanted to be alone with her grief, to give it its head, to let it crush her; and Jenny, with her damnable Welsh obstinacy, was steadily denying her this luxury. And what right had she to come between Stella and her tragedy? Her last emotion before she went to sleep was her indignation with Jenny.

It took two days for the first numbing shock to pass, and during that time she was certain that she wanted to die. She could see no hope at all. Beyond that point there was only darkness. She would soon be thirty-three. She had nobody – except Jenny – to turn to. *He* had treated her inhumanly, treacherously, barbarously, and unless it was to die she could think of no adequate reaction. She tried very hard to die. She was resentful when she found she couldn't. She had decided that it would be unsatisfactory to give nature any assistance, and apart from eating very little, tried to will herself into a decline. But at the end of two days she was ravenously hungry and what was more, she wanted to talk about the injury Justin had done her.

So she ate, and talked, and anger replaced the sense of shock. She forgot that she wanted to die and meditated a more satisfying revenge. A magnificent scene had suggested itself – dramatically, she would interrupt Justin's wedding: at the point where the clergyman enquired for impediments she would throw herself passionately between Justin and that woman. She spent many hours elaborating this incident, adjusting each detail with the eye of a true novelist. It didn't occur to her until later that she never intended to act it, but that it would make a likely sequence in some book yet to be written. Then she caught herself smiling. It was feeble, but it was a smile.

Jenny had shielded her from the papers and her mail for some days, but in the end her curiosity made her hunt for the latter. Everyone had seen the announcement, and there must have been some press comment; she didn't know, then, that Jenny had resolutely seen off the reporters. Jenny had also fixed the phone. All Stella's calls were going through to Miss Williams. For several days Stella had enjoyed an existence which was hermetically sealed from the world. She'd had a fresh fit of tears when she began to discover these things, for really she'd been beastly to Jenny, she had behaved like a spoiled brat. And Jenny, almost a stranger, had taken it all in her stride; without a moment's hesitation she had put herself at Stella's service.

'Tomorrow is Sunday again, my dear. We'll go for an outing after lunch.'

'Oh no, Jenny. I couldn't!' Stella stared at her in dismay. She had been clinging to the flat as to a last foothold on dry land, she hadn't yet dared to contemplate her re-entry into the world.

'You have been indoors a week. You are beginning to look quite peaked.'

'No, Jenny, not yet. I'm bound to run into someone.'

'Well that won't kill you, and they're keeping a skiff for us. I rang the man at Kingston. We're having an outing on the river.'

And, tearfully, she let Jenny cajole her out of the flat, and they drove in Jenny's ancient Mini to the Bridge Boatyard in Kingston. It was a sultry June day; everybody was on the river. To Hampton Court and beyond there were streams of skiffs, punts, dinghies. The sun was almost unbearable. Jenny had forgotten about sunshades. By the time they had sculled up to the eyot they were content to get off the river, and finding a retreat behind the eyot, they slid the skiff into it. But even there it was hot, under the ceiling of low willow branches. The air was motionless and the water looked muddy and thick-flowing. They lay prone among the cushions, listening to the oars of passing boats, with sometimes a launch going by to set the skiff rocking and swaying.

'Well, my dear, and what are are you going to do?'

After a long silence Jenny had turned her head to look at Stella. She had large, solemn eyes which, oddly, seemed to envelope one, and just then perspiration was beading on her pretty freckled nose.

Stella shook her head. 'I don't know. I just don't know.'

'How about your people, now?'

'No, I couldn't go to them.'

Stella's father was a country GP who had a practice in Somerset. They had never got on very well and there had been a row when she left home. His favourite was her elder sister; Elizabeth had sided with him in the row.

'Have you no friends, then?'

'No, not them.' She couldn't bear the thought of people who knew about it.

'Nobody at all where you could stay for a bit?'

'Nobody at all. I just want to be alone.'

Jenny had nodded seriously as though she found that quite intelligible. She had reached up over her head and plucked a twitch of the willow. With this she'd played for a minute or so, unravelling the golden skin, before saying, very carefully:

'Would you know Simon Lea-Stephens?'

'Lea-Stephens?' Stella thought a moment, then realised that she did. 'I shook hands with him once. We met at a launching party.'

'Well, you know, we're his publishers, and I know him quite well. He's made a terrible lot of money. It's that musical that's done it.'

Stella shrugged without comment. Lea-Stephens was nothing to her. She had read one of his books, but only out of curiosity. He was not a 'serious' writer and Stella herself was deadly serious: she had not been at all surprised when he had branched out into musicals. With Woody Woodmancott, the composer, he had written *The Golden Girl*.

'He lives in Norfolk, you know, when he isn't in town. A marvellous place he has, too. It is near one of the Broads.'

'You're not suggesting he'd lend it to me?'

'Oh no! I know he wouldn't. He'll be going down there himself in a week or two. He spends the summer there, you know, with his guests and various people. But he has a cottage down there as well, and I just happen to know it's empty.'

'I don't want to be on someone's doorstep.'

'No, and you wouldn't be. It's a good mile from the house. It's a place on its own, and it's got a summerhouse by the Broad – ideal, it is, and right by itself.'

Jenny was too good a psychologist to urge the idea. Having planted it she left it to grow, and returned to peeling her willow-wand. Stella lay with her eyes closed, her head cradled in her hands; thinking, thinking, trying to plan some possible future. She couldn't continue living in Kensington, that was the one clear thing. Her loathing for Kensington was suddenly physical. It made her shudder as she lay there. Kensington meant her crowd, the people she'd introduced Justin to – pitying and sneering: she couldn't take either. And everywhere it would be the same, wherever they knew her, whether they showed it or not they would be thinking, examining her. It was too much to bear. There would need to be an interval. She would have to go away for a spell, for a year perhaps. And that being so, where better to bury herself than Norfolk: who of her set ever went there, except the Carters, who came from King's Lynn?

Restively she stirred her legs: 'My God, I'm thirsty! Can't we get a drink somewhere?'

'We passed a pub as we came along.'

Jenny said no more about the cottage or Stella's plans for the future. Stella was rather sorry she didn't. She felt she would like to have been persuaded.

4

And she was persuaded, in the end.

Jenny, with Welsh slyness, took the business quietly in hand, getting in touch with Lea-Stephens' secretary and eventually with Lea-Stephens. Three days later Stella had a letter from him, beautifully written on monogrammed notepaper; it was tactful, it was cordial, one felt it came from a most sincere friend. Simon expressed himself frankly about Stella's misfortune and appreciated that she would be glad to get away from London. He was happy to be able to offer her Heron Cottage, near Barford Broad, and hoped she would do him the honour of becoming his tenant. If she would meet him for a drink they could settle up the business.

'You're the devil, Jenny!'

Stella had dressed in a restrained, tailored costume, and for the first time since the catastrophe she had made up her face. She used a little gardenia perfume and pinned violets in her buttonhole, chose an unobtrusive hat and carried her slim, shepherd's crook umbrella. In a suitably subdued way she knew she looked attractive. Jenny's eye had run over her approvingly when she came down to the taxi. Stella felt a little guilty, like a widow gone prematurely gay; but she was meeting Simon at his select club and she could scarcely have done less.

He was waiting for her in the club lounge and had his secretary with him. He introduced her – Jill Shore, an auburn-haired girl with a boyish face. Then she went off to type some letters and Simon ordered their drinks. It was early, and they had the lounge pretty well to themselves.

'Call me Simon, for the sake of brevity.'

He soon broke down any awkwardness. He was off at once on an amusing tale about his collaborator, Woody. His eyes were watchful behind their smiling but she didn't find that offensive. They were appreciative, too. They took in her figure, which her suit flattered.

'Have you been to the Broads before?'

'Once, yes. But I was quite a child.'

'You'll like it there. It drips with poetry. It's got a voluptuous, feminine beauty. There's nowhere else a bit like it and once you're bitten you have to go back. Can you sail a boat, by the way?'

'Yes, a dinghy. I can manage that.'

'There's an assortment of boats at Lazy Waters, so you can borrow a dinghy or what you like.'

Simon was plainly an enthusiast when it came to the Broads

and his grey eyes sparkled as he spoke of their attractions. His 'school', he told her, had been Gresham's, only a stone's-throw from the Broads, and as a member of the school sailing club he had come to know them young. He had an especial charm while in the flush of his enthusiasm. Soon Stella began to think that she had judged him rather harshly. Because he was a 'pop' writer she had been automatically deprecating, not allowing that one could be likeable while falling short of divine genius. Simon was infinitely likeable.

'Would you like a longish lease?'

'I hadn't . . . I'm not sure . . .'

In a panic, she realised suddenly that she was liable to go to pieces. She was living on a sort of tight-rope on which Jenny had managed to set her, but the least little pressure was likely to upset her balance. Fortunately, Simon appeared not to notice.

'You'd like to see it first, I expect. I'll get on to Jill to write to Mrs Allcock. You can have it as soon as you like.'

'Oh, in a week or so, perhaps . . .'

'Jill will give you a key, then you can go down when you're ready.'

She finished her drink and left as soon as she decently could. It was ridiculous, but a howling fit had been right at her elbow. At one moment she had been feeling confident and certain of herself, the next a prop seemed to have fallen out and the abyss to have opened beneath her. She hailed a taxi, then changed her mind: it would never do for her to give in! Instead, she walked along the pavement until she came to a café. There she ordered Jenny's remedy, a cup of strong, sweet tea, and sipping it tried to take a firm hold on her emotions.

She had no intention of giving up her flat. It had been her home for three years and it represented her independence. It was not an imposing *pied-à-terre* but it was comfortable and convenient, and by good luck she was in funds due to selling the serial rights of her book. Thus her packing didn't take long. It took her longer to resolve to do it. After the interview with Simon she was filled with doubts about the wisdom of the move. Jenny rallied her when she could, but of course she spent the day at her office, and often she came in from work to find Stella snivelling into a pillow. That move had something fundamental about it, something which she couldn't put into words; it was cutting deep into roots which Justin's treachery hadn't touched.

'After this, I'm going to be old . . .'

'Don't be a foolish woman, Stella.'

To Jenny this was probably the most trying part of the business. She needed to nag Stella constantly, yet to be for ever cheering her up. It required the temperament of a saint and the obstinacy of the devil, and just occasionally Jenny's temper was unequal to the task.

'People have been jilted before, and lived.'

'That's unfair! I wasn't just jilted.'

'It's the name we give it in Wales.'

'I hate you Jenny. I hate Wales too.'

'Well then, be a woman. Face up to things a bit. I'd be ashamed to let any man make a fool of me like that.'

'You wait. You'll find out what it's like to be jilted.'

She made up her mind finally over a week after the interview. The weather, which till then had been uncertain, suddenly turned fair. It made the town look shabby, the buildings across the street seemed tired; a malaise had settled on everything and even the air seemed second-hand. They made the trip in Jenny's Mini on the last weekend in June. Stella clung to Jenny till the last – she would like to have removed her too. When they arrived at the cottage they bustled about and scraped together a meal of sorts, and Jenny was not allowed to depart before she had promised to return to spend a weekend. When she drove off, Stella stood in the road, watching the Mini till it was out of sight. The convalescence was over. Now Stella had to stand alone.

5

In the morning she discovered what her feelings of the evening had prevented, namely that Heron Cottage was as perfect a retreat as a forlorn damsel might ask for. She had received some details of it from Simon, but these hadn't really registered; she had remembered only that it was on the mains and had a bath and was free from neighbours. Now she was at leisure to take it in and she was thrilled with delight by it. After her three years in Kensington she seemed to have entered a foreign land.

The cottage was situated on a by-road about a mile from Alderford village, standing back behind trees that almost hid it from passers-by. It was single-storied, built of flint and rusty brick, the roof thatched with reed thatch and the windows furnished with green shutters. It wasn't large, but it was delectable. The rooms had been decorated with taste. No attempt had been made to simulate original furniture; what there was was modern and plain, but the sort of plainness that hinted at quality. There was a modern kitchen and a hot-water system. Big windows had been added to the principal room. A touch of luxury was in the bathroom, which possessed a sunken bath, and in the bedroom odd corners had been turned into fitted cupboards and a fitted wardrobe. In all, it must have cost Simon a great deal of money, and Stella couldn't help wondering what his object had been in spending it. He had let it to her at a rent which she now saw was purely nominal.

After admiring it, and revelling in the crazy-paved garden, she suddenly remembered that the cottage was only part of the attraction. Somewhere through the trees awaited the summer-house and the Broad, and she set out at once to take the measure of these delights. She found the path behind the cottage. It led windingly into a plantation, then down into an alder carr where, on either hand, one saw pools and strange marsh plants. She smelled again the peculiar fragrance that seemed to epitomise the Broads: that warm odour of peat and bruised mint and aquatic plants, and among the rushes surrounding a pool she saw her first live heron; at her approach it rose lazily, dangling long green legs. It wasn't far to the summerhouse and this morning she could have wished it further, for the sight of the carr, and particularly its smell, took her back several years. She remembered the sun of a distant summer when she had been there before, a hoydenish schoolgirl; until now she had completely forgotten this haunting fragrance. It came back to her like a song.

As with the cottage the summerhouse exceeded her expectation; it was so unlike what she had imagined, and yet so exactly right. It was of thatched timber and plaster and consisted of two stories, the lower one a wet boathouse in which a sailing dinghy was already moored. Some outside stairs led to the upper floor, which comprised a room about twelve feet square, furnished with a bamboo table, some cane chairs and a wicker couch. It opened on to a veranda from which the view was extensive, and she leaned her elbows on the rail while she paused to take it in.

The wild luxuriance was bewildering, and struck her senses with amazement. The scene began at her very feet and stretched away to an uncertain distance. An arm of the Broad, less than a hundred yards wide, bounded by reeds and carrs of alder, reached a quarter of a mile from the summerhouse into the parent water beyond. Its beginnings were confused by reedbeds and by islands of spiky rushes, so that it was screened from the Broad, an expanse of which could be glimpsed over reeds. And this private, secret lake was a living bed of water-lilies. Their golden-shadowed white stars floated there by the hundred. On the placid open water, among the sibilant reed-stems, between the rushy islands, they bloomed and bloomed. A number of yellow lilies grew among them and one could detect their languorous perfume; swallows hawked above them, and dragon-flies shimmered their metallic wings. Then, above the reed-tops close to her, soared a pair of swallowtail butterflies, so large and so handsome that they made Stella catch her breath.

She resolved on the spot that she would do her writing in the summerhouse, and almost at the same instant that she would begin a new book. She would work, she would work hard, that was the proper way to get rid of Justin; and if her book crucified a Justin-figure, well, it wouldn't be the worse for that. She went back to the cottage with her mind made up. She marvelled that she hadn't thought of beginning a book earlier. Now that she did her vexed future seemed to be wondrously clarified; it was simple. She would write books on the veranda of that fabulous summerhouse . . .

For the rest of the day she attended to the duties of settling in, but her solitude was buoyed by the idea of the book she was going to write. Her morbid broodings over Justin were given a new and healthier turn: they were now the raw material from which she was shaping the pages ahead. On the second day she took her typewriter and gear to the summerhouse and, using a pen, began work on a synopsis of the novel. The scenery was perhaps a little distracting to one who was used to a Kensington skyline, but she was a professional, she had learned the knack of establishing a routine. She worked doggedly, to the clock. She had more trouble than she expected. Despite the metamorphosis she was experiencing, her material gave her pain. There were times when she stared at the notebook while silent tears rolled down her cheeks and, despite her best intentions, she couldn't get on with the job. It would be a cruel book to write, but she felt incapable of writing anything else.

By the end of the week she had advanced to the writing and then at last she was more at peace. There was a power to soothe in the steady creation and the familiar exercise of her skill. Also, she was pleased by her unviolated solitude, for, except tradesmen, nobody called at the cottage. She had made one excursion into Alderford to arrange her supplies, but after that her only communication had been by phone. In fact she had seen but one other person, a rather picturesque figure who had rowed in from the Broad. He gave the name of Sam Fulcher and wanted to do some gardening for her, a service which he assured her he had done for her predecessor. She'd been amused by the fellow.

'Who had the cottage here before me?'

'Oh, one of them actress women – Miss Lorraine, she called herself.'

He had remained sitting in his boat, an ancient, patched double-ender, and had paddled away with slow dignity after she'd told him she would think about it. He seemed as natural a phenomenon as a coot or a waterhen and his rough clothes and leisurely motions exactly suited the spirit of the place.

Another denizen of the Broad, but one who kept his distance, was a fisherman who occupied a white-painted houseboat. It was moored out in the rush islands, just visible from her veranda, and she often saw him sitting there and sometimes caught the flash of a fish in his landing net. There were passing sails also, white, tan, blue or dark red, and throbbing motor-cruisers which held their course in the distance. She had just a window on the world, it went its way to confirm her privacy. Her troubled soul had found a haven in which to rest and calm itself.

Then, on Sunday, the phone rang:

'Stella, dear –?'

She'd forgotten Simon. In a fluttering panic she remembered that he was due to be down there, too. At the same moment, by the tone of his voice, she realised that something was expected of her: she was not going to be allowed to remain in her desired oblivion.

'You have settled in, have you?'

'Yes . . . yes. It's beautiful.'

'Good.' He gave a little, complacent chuckle. 'I thought you might be surprised. I rather pique myself on the cottage, I planned the conversion myself. It was a terrible drum when I bought the property. Somebody's gamekeeper used to live in it.'

'I like it very much.'

'Good. Then I've got myself a tenant. But I really rang up to ask if you'll come over for supper. There's only one or two of us, so you don't have to fuss. I'll pick you up at half-past six. It'll give us time for a drink.'

She made an attempt to excuse herself. She was furious at her weakness; she knew she ought to be able to say no without stooping to hypocrisy.

'But, my dear, it's only a meal, and you can leave as soon as you like.'

She found herself stumbling into an acceptance and then was furious all over again.

Damn! Damn! Damn! She sat cursing silently after he'd rung off. For want of that simple, easy negative she had let him trample on her privacy. Having done it once he would do it again, there would be no end to the intrusions; she had visions of her life plagued by a steady round of invitations and visits. And this, after only a week, a single week of blissful solitude, at the end of which she had only just established the necessary rhythm of her daily life . . .

She had a mind to pack her things and leave, and nothing but the effort required prevented her from doing it.

6

But she was ready when Simon arrived, and she had consciously chosen a dress which became her ('Stella Rushton, you're a fool, you're a fool, Stella Rushton'). She was waiting for him in the garden, thoughtfully posed on its rustic bench, and she let him get out of the car and come up the path in search of her. Simon gave her his warming smile.

'You're looking a picture, Stella my sweet.'

She smiled back with wan acceptance ('I'm only showing you I'm not dead yet').

He lingered for a few moments to run a fond eye over his property, then picking up her wrap he escorted her to his car. It was a powder-blue Jaguar with cream leather upholstery, and boasted an array of auxiliary lamps and several badges on the front. Simon drove it slowly and caressingly. He was obviously very proud of it. He had perhaps driven something less imposing before the affluent era of *The Golden Girl*.

'This is Iriston, you see – you are not far from Lazy Waters. Don't look for a village, because there isn't one here. We get our supplies from Alderford – Iriston is just a name. There's the church and three cottages, two bungalows, and me.'

They had driven a short distance along the by-road from Alderford, which was flanked on one side by fields of wheat and on the other by plantations and carrs; now the road came to an end by the tower of a flint church, and beyond lay the narrow river that flowed from the Broad. Simon took a turn to the left along a springy cinder track. It was bordered by pollard willows and riotous marsh vegetation. Soon, towering among taller willows, one saw high roofs of crisp thatch, and there appeared two wrought-iron gates into the design of which was woven: Lazy Waters.

'The finest house on the Broads, my dear.'

Simon grinned at her boyishly. He knew his vanity, he seemed to say, and you are welcome to smile at it. He parked the Jaguar on the drive in a position that was decorative, then helped Stella out, closing the doors with care. She looked about her with interest. The house was truly a fine one; built of the same materials as her summerhouse, it showed how strikingly they could be used. The plan was in the shape of a cross, which gave the house interest and mass, and also provided a classic foundation for a display of the thatcher's craft. This had been lavished on it with splendour; one looked first at the beautiful roofs. They had wonderfully carved and scalloped ridges and were moulded sweetly over semi-circular attic windows. A spacious veranda ran entirely round the building, having four separate flights of steps to the drive and lawns below. The windows were large, timber-framed and latticed. A golden weather-vane swung elegantly above the thatch. Standing among tall, natural willows, fenced by azaleas and rhododendrons, it had the air of a summer pavilion of some legendary prince of Cathay.

Simon led her round the house to admire the front lawn and

25

the gardens. The former had the shaven carpet-like perfection reserved for lawns grown over peat. It had sidebeds vivid with begonias and a great variety of roses, and was bordered by weeping willows and screens of dumpy dwarf azaleas. Beyond the lawn, past more tall willows, one saw the river with its traffic of pleasure boats, and to the right a spacious wet boathouse with matching thatch and a kindred weather-vane.

'It was built by a stockbroker with more taste than most.'

Simon kept close beside her, his hand on her elbow. Once or twice she caught him looking at her, half-anxiously, half-thoughtfully; she couldn't define the look or decide what it signified. He was being careful to steer clear of any reference to her troubles.

'There's a bit of land that goes with it, though it's mostly fen. It takes in the bottom end of the Broad as far as the cottage. The cottage is additional. It was going for a song. I thought it would round off the property nicely and make it easy to oblige a friend.'

'Did the stockbroker build my summerhouse?'

'Oh yes. You can see, it's in the same style as the house. It's a pleasant spot for a picnic and to keep a boat for fishing, and I believe there used to be a path from it to the house. But now it's all grown up. The place was neglected when I bought it.'

'It doesn't look neglected.'

'I had a golden wand, my dear.'

Beside the waterfront, along which ran an immaculate piled heading, they came to a seat where it was pleasant to sit watching the passing boats. His guests, Simon explained, had gone for a trip on the Broad, and he brooded thoughtfully for a moment, his handsome eyes fixed on the water.

'We're not a large party this time. In fact, there are only five of us. Plus Jill, of course. And my nephew, Keith.'

'Do I know any of them?'

'No, I don't think so, so I'll put you in the picture while we're sinking a drink.'

He ushered her back to the house and through French windows into a lounge, a large, restful room panelled with silver-grained wood. He sat her down on a settee and chose a bottle from a cabinet. Then he poured them sherries in two smoky glasses and brought them over and sat down beside her.

'Now, there's Woody, the one and only, who you will like as a matter of course. He's taller than a church steeple and makes me feel quite a mannikin. He has a large, haggard face set in a sort of Slav melancholy, but in fact he comes from Melbourne and his parents hailed from Cornwall. Then there's Jeff, Jeff Simpson, our tame choreographer. You'll place him up Bradford way the moment he opens his mouth. And Dawn le Fay, *née* Molly Jimpson, who played Lulu in the *Girl*. She's a rising young thing with all the right statistics. And then there's Glynda.'

Simon broke off to inspect her, quizzically. Stella received the impression that he wanted to say something which he found difficult to put into words. At last he shrugged elegant shoulders:

'You're another writer and I'm going to be frank. It would be a pity if you and I couldn't talk without hypocrisy. I'm a bachelor, you know, and I prefer it that way. And bachelors are like other men. I sometimes think they are more so.'

'You mean that Glynda —'

'She's my very good friend. She's an actress who had a part in my play, *The Stars*. She admits to thirty, and she isn't near the top of her profession. Between ourselves, she is much better suited to being someone's friend.'

It was frank indeed, and Simon was watching every reaction. In a way Stella felt flattered to be the recipient of such a confidence. He had wanted to tell her while not finding it easy; he seemed to be appealing to her to accept his moral obliquity.

'I think I may have heard her name.'

'Glynda Davis. She was mostly in rep. A brown-eyed brunette with a wide mouth and an oval chin. Played character parts, second leads and the like.'

'And you're – fond of each other?'

Simon appeared to relax. He took a long sip from his glass

and grinned at her with a flash of wickedness.

'I'm not in love with her, if that's what you mean. I'm an egoist to the core. I was spoiled as a boy. But I'm fond of her, yes, and she's fond of me too. Then one day we'll get bored and I shall use my influence to find her a part. I'm a bachelor pure and simple, and one has to face facts.'

'That is quite heartless, you know.'

'I do know. I am heartless. It's a relief now and then to be able to admit it. In the common way I'm a hypocrite, like everybody else. But I try to be generous to make up for my other failings.'

She found herself smiling and shrugging her assent – it was fair: he didn't pretend to have virtues he lacked. She could imagine Simon's mistresses departing without rancour. They had not been duped . . . unlike herself.

'Well, I hope you're good to her.'

'Yes,' Simon was serious. 'One has to arrange a certain order in one's life, don't you agree? One is compounded of a set of elements and it is no use fighting them. The true art is to strike a harmony, to accept with grace what we can't alter.'

'And Glynda represents one of your acceptances.'

'Exactly. I accept the need that Glynda supplies. I don't call it love or anything exalted, but it's there, and necessary to be taken care of. And I make the best concession that my nature allows. I would not be a better person if I tried to fight it. I would be irritable and bearish and my work would probably suffer, and I would likely be the victim of all sorts of odd delusions. And so I have my Glynda, and all goes well.'

Was it a sermon? Stella tried to read his smiling, frank eyes. If it was, he had succeeded in putting it over very cleverly. Only the reference to 'odd delusions' had touched a chord that was possibly personal, and it had fitted quite naturally into the context of what he was saying. She couldn't be certain. She had a lot to learn about Simon.

'Just a minute, my dear. I must have a word with Ruby.'

A maid in an overall had come to the door, and Simon rose to attend to her. Stella sank into a dreamy brooding over the glass in her hand. A minute or so later Simon returned, accompanied by a tall young man wearing shorts. Simon was saying:

'This is Keith, my dear. He's my nephew from Cambridge.'

7

And after all it wasn't quite such an ordeal as she had expected, she neither burst into tears nor ran away directly after the meal. On the contrary, she was surprised to find herself taking a normal interest in things, amused to meet new people and ready to observe and speculate about them. Everyone seemed pleased to meet her in their various ways. There were no impertinent queries about herself and Justin. Indeed, she came soon to realise that they probably knew nothing about it – they were theatre people, an airtight society; they knew nothing and cared less about what went on behind the footlights. She didn't know whether she was a little hurt to be so thoroughly unimportant.

As Simon had predicted, she took at once to Woody Woolmancott, a big gangling man with a mop of straggly grey hair. He had twinkling green eyes to offset the gaunt lines of his face, and a careless, lazy way of speaking, as though words dragged far behind his thoughts. Jeff Simpson she thought she liked too though he was more difficult to understand. About forty, he had narrow, sallow features and eyes that were tense and unsmiling. She saw that he was much struck by Dawn Le Fay (née Molly Jimpson). She also saw that Dawn was determined to be discouraging. Dawn was a doll-faced blonde who went in for cleavages to her navel; her talk was inane but she was far from simple, and she undoubtedly knew where she was going.

With Glynda, Stella had to admit herself disappointed: she had imagined that Simon's mistress would be more exotic, more interesting. Instead she was introduced to a rather drab-faced woman, voluptuous certainly, but not otherwise distinguished. The chin was square rather than oval and a sulky expression hinted at temper. Glynda made a smile for Stella and shook hands perfunctorily, then glanced quickly back at Simon to see which of them his eyes were on.

'It was charming on the Broad, darling. A pity we had to go without you.'

'I was quite busy, darling. But there will be other days.'

Simon smiled at her sincerely. He kissed her tenderly on the cheek.

These people, along with Jill Shore, who had learned the art of conforming, made a circle of similar tastes and of fairly harmonious temperaments. They had their all-absorbing subject which had never been known to flag, they had comparable interests in it, they responded to one another. They had their moral tone in common. They adored exchanging smutty gossip. In some ways amusingly naïve, they were in others cynically sophisticated. To them it was a matter of course that Simon and Glynda should sleep together but they would probably have been honestly shocked to learn of Stella's indifference to the theatre. The one was a commonplace of the profession, the other would have made them blush for her.

But there was an odd man out: Keith was neither of them nor with them. A nervous stranger, he hovered anonymously on the periphery of the circle. During supper he was seated by Stella and at first she scarcely noticed him; he was silent, apparently abstracted, and had no more conversation than his chair. She did her best:

'Did you get through your exams all right?'

He flushed under his tan, his eyes meeting hers uneasily. He had fair, reddish hair and a nose that tended to a button. His eyes were a smoky hazel. He had a small, ripe mouth.

'I think so. The results are not through yet.'

'What are you going into?'

'Oh . . . industry, I expect.'

'You're not attracted by research?'

'No . . . I don't know.'

'It's more interesting, I should think.'

'Yes, but . . . nothing's settled, yet.'

He was trembling, the poor lamb, and he was blushing to his ears. She felt a little thrill of pleasure and amusement tempered. Surely he hadn't fallen for her, and at such short notice – with the Le Fay in the offing to supply competition? She looked him over thoughtfully: he certainly seemed agitated.

'Anyway, you've got a nice long vacation now.'

'Yes. Till October.'

'Will you spend part of it abroad?'

'Yes . . . I don't know. Perhaps Paris.'

'It's the wrong time for Paris.'

'Well . . . I don't know.'

She was conscious suddenly of Simon watching the pair of them and of a stab of displeasure at being thus observed. She turned away from Keith abruptly and gave her attention to her plate. From the corner of her eye she thought she could see Simon give a faint shrug.

They had coffee in the lounge with its view towards the river. A grand piano stood in one corner and Woody went to take possession of it. His long body, perched on the stool, seemed to dwarf the large instrument, and he leaned about at grotesque angles as he softly and brilliantly played.

'Woody can never get past a piano.'

Simon brought his coffee beside her. He offered her a cigarette from a slim, monogrammed gold case. Glynda was chatting with Jeff and a bored-looking Jill Shore. Dawn was sprawled by herself on the settee. Her pretty face wore a blank expression.

'Is he playing something I should know?'

Simon shook his head. 'Not Woody. He plays it straight from his inside. He'll go on like that until someone kicks him.'

'You mean he makes it up as he goes along?'

'He does just that. Then, one day, he writes it down. Woody has a memory like an elephant's. He never forgets a note he plays.'

'But that's remarkable.'

'Oh, I don't know. Some people have it and some haven't.

31

Keith can remember reams of poetry – he's the envy of Dawn, who fluffs every other line.'

Remembering Keith, Stella glanced about her and found him sitting at a distance, with a book. More than ever he seemed a total stranger, determined to shut himself away from the others. She now noticed that he had changed since he had been introduced to her, when he was wearing a grubby sports shirt and even grubbier shorts; he had put on some fawn trousers with the memory of a crease in them, a neat open-neck shirt and a Cumberland tweed jacket. Apparently he didn't smoke. He looked appealingly innocent. He had an engaging frown or scowl as he gazed at the printed page. With rather mixed feelings she identified the book as one of her own. It was a collection of silly poems which, like many writers, she had produced in her nonage.

'Didn't I tell you that he admired your work?' Simon was grinning amiably at her. 'When I told him who I had for a tenant he was most impressed, believe me. He went into Norwich and bought two of your books he hadn't read.'

'Isn't he a little bit out of things at Lazy Waters?'

'Of course he is my dear. He's never met the like before. But we all have to grow up. Life isn't a succession of lecture periods. I'm hoping that his stay here may prove educational.'

'But he is so utterly different from the rest of you.'

Simon cocked a humorous eyebrow. 'Do I detect a note of censure? But that's all to the good you know, the young man needs a rub of sophistication. Besides, he enjoys being here apart from the society we offer. He adores sailing and fishing and messing about in boats. He was born under Cancer, which gives him a penchant for the water – he swims like a seal and represents his college. No, he likes Lazy Waters, and perhaps not the less because of its inmates. They are very strange and disquieting – they are very good for Keith.'

'You will never make him like one of yourselves.'

'Again that gentle note of reproof! And heaven forbid, say I, that Keith should ever become a theatre type. But he has a balance to be redressed. He has been living too much out of the world. Wouldn't it be educative, for example, if he had a little fling with Dawn?'

Stella was silent for a space. She was trying to weigh the morals of this. She found the idea distasteful but couldn't assign an immediate reason for it.

'I don't think Dawn would find him amusing.'

'So much the better, he would learn the hard way. But what makes you so certain that Dawn is difficult to amuse? Take a look around the room and see who is sitting alone. You can discount Woody – he's never alone with a piano.'

Stella looked, and saw. Dawn still lay on the settee. She was draped languishingly, seductively, with a knee waving in the air. Jeff Simpson had his eye on her but Dawn was ignoring him: her head was turned towards the windows, where sat Keith with Stella's book. No interpreter was needed.

'She's not his sort. She's too exotic.'

Simon chuckled. 'You think she'll scare him? She lacks subtlety, I agree. But that's what makes it rather interesting. It should bear watching if it develops.'

'You're a more likely customer yourself.'

'I kiss your hand, but keep your voice down.'

When the conversation became more general however Dawn showed no reluctance to taking part, and an hour of theatre talk slipped by without her once glancing in Keith's direction. Stella found herself keeping a close eye on them, especially Dawn, who puzzled her. Dawn had a sullen expression; she was bitchy to Jeff Simpson, and suspiciously neutral towards Simon. Had there been a row at some time? Stella wondered what it had been about. Perhaps it concerned some professional matter about which she could guess nothing. It could scarcely have been over Keith when Simon's attitude was so accommodating, but Glynda's jealousy might have sparked something and provided a motive for Dawn's behaviour. 'I kiss your hand, but keep your voice down.' Had she divined Simon's secret?

She quietly detached herself from the group and moved to a chair near Keith.

'I couldn't help seeing what it is you're reading.'

He looked up eagerly. 'I've read them before, but . . .'

She smiled. 'Now you want to compare the poems with the person.'

He was absurdly young and puppyish, a man animal in the ferment of his spring. His vulnerability gave her a pang, he seemed so undefended and woundable. He was taller than Simon, bigger and clumsier, his shoulders broad and his body well-fleshed, but he lacked the symmetry of feature that made his uncle so photogenic. Yet he had his own good looks. His features knitted well together. They gave an impression of character, of ardent sincerity. When he was older they would probably fine a little and then he would be regarded as handsome; now they depended on their bloom and on the coltish charm of youth. He was about the same age as Dawn, but she had several centuries start on him.

'So what do you think of us, the poems and me?'

'They . . . they've got passion. I don't know how to express it.'

'Most of them were written when I was your age.'

'Yes . . . I understand. You were in love with someone.'

'But I wasn't.' Stella was taken aback. Her published poems hadn't been amatory. Of these she had written quite a few but her natural reserve had prevented her from including them. Entitled *Floating Vistas*, her collection had been mostly poems of mood and place.

'Yes, you must have been. In love with someone. They sound so full of it. So full of . . . yearning.'

'I was in love with love then. And that's not an uncommon malady.'

'I can't think you wrote them . . . well, just cold.'

She laughed in amusement, because that was just how she had written them. She had always planned her work and her poetry along with the rest. She had never described an emotion which had not been recollected in tranquillity; she had seized a mood for each poem but she had evoked it by taking thought.

'I'm not a very good poet.'

'But you are. You are really.'

34

'It's kind of you to say so and I'm enchanted by the compliment.'

'You make one feel and understand. You show them new ways of experiencing things. I wish I could tell you . . . after reading them, one knows you.'

'Not too well, I hope!'

'But it's true, you know.'

'I shall have to be more careful what I publish in the future.'

They finished up silent and looking at each other, he staring defencelessly and Stella determinedly amused. She knew now, quite certainly, that Keith had fallen for her, and she was resolved to keep the callow young man in his place. To do other would be ridiculous: there was over a decade between them. She wasn't old enough to be his mother but she would have made a distinctly elder sister.

'You write poetry, Simon says.'

'Yes . . . at least, I try.'

'A poet is a writer in embryo you know.'

He stared a little at this heresy. 'But I've always understood –'

'A poem is the first and easier form of literary expression.'

He looked bewildered; he began to say something about William Faulkner. But she brushed him aside, changing the subject deftly. She was adept at applying a snub, she had a wicked touch with one, she could keep a man in continual discomfort without ever exposing herself to retaliation. And yet, in the end, he completely disarmed her:

'I've been thinking . . . you look so much like Jane Austen in that portrait.'

She did, she knew she did; she was almost guilty of a blush. She was silenced and for some moments pretended to be absorbed by Woody's playing.

Simon drove her back to the cottage. She realised then how tired she was. For several hours she had lived on her nerves and now she was half-inclined to snivel. Her mind would run away to Justin, however hard she tried to stop it, she felt it was unfair that she should be so wretched when the people she had been with were so complacent. She grudged them their petty jealousies. These seemed very desirable emotions.

'Well, my dear, I hope we amused you with our tantrums and tattle.'

'Thank you Simon. I enjoyed it.'

'You must make a habit of us. By the bye, I think you've put poor Dawn's nose out of joint. I'm rather sorry about that. I would like to have seen how Keith handled it.'

'Keith is a silly young man.'

'Dear Stella, we are all silly. Men are very foolish creatures until women take them in hand. But it's an inimitable process and I wouldn't have it otherwise.'

'You've been spoiled by too many women.'

'But it's the first one who's important.'

She found herself laughing as she gave him her hand. He brushed it with his lips, and she went into the cottage.

8

She was tired, but she didn't go directly to bed. She lay smoking for a while on the studio couch in the cottage's living room. Although it was eleven it was scarcely dark so she didn't put on the light, and as the night was mild and still, she set her French windows wide open. Then she lay with her thoughts, watching the tip of the cigarette smoulder; she discovered a great deal to think about and not all of it was painful.

She liked Simon very much; it was easy to see why women fell for him. He had distinction himself and he made a woman feel distinguished. He was intelligent and observant. He had tact and good manners. He communicated a poise while being quite prepared to laugh at himself. He was probably not wholly sincere, but one didn't take exception to that; it was the necessary price that one had to pay for charm and politeness. In an imperfect world there were not many Simons and it was worthwhile to compound for their sins: she couldn't help contrasting him with Justin. Both were egotists, but one was a hypocrite.

Woody she liked, with his rueful face; Jeff Simpson she had yet to make up her mind about. She was intrigued by Glynda, she was curious about Jill, and she decided that she was too wise to take an active dislike to Dawn. And Keith, of course – the poor angel, with his poetry! She hoped that Keith would find a really nice girl to hang his sonnets on. He was terribly sensitive, she could see, he could be hurt all too easily; he needed firm but gentle handling in his emotional debut. She tried to picture the proper girl for him and toyed with the idea of Jenny. She held Jenny in high esteem and could answer for her generosity. But wasn't Jenny a little hard, a little too much of a ward-sister – wouldn't she affront his romantic feelings with her implacable common-sense? He needed someone more like himself, with a readier response to the subtle nuances: one who had been through the experience herself and could vividly remember its aches and pains. But a girl with these qualities was a little difficult to imagine, for unless in maturity they were not easy to come by. An older person seemed indicated, perhaps a woman in her late twenties, somewhat dedicated, Stella hoped, and likely to behave with disinterest. It was a situation requiring a paragon and she admitted doubts as to whether he would find one.

For half an hour she lay thinking about anything but Justin, then she rose, locked the French windows, and went upstairs to undress. She lit the light on the dressing table, and stood for some moments examining herself – she had always a critical eye for the weak points of her person. She thought she would probably diet and take an inch off her stomach. It would be foolish to run to seed merely on account of Justin. She was pleased enough with the rest, her figure had always been passable, and she had a good waist and hips and her legs were shapely and supple. Her bust gave her no qualms, it was on the large side but quite firm. She had elegantly sloping shoulders and just the neck to go with them. She studied her face; in this light it was astonishingly Austenesque. The cheeks were rounded, the chin decisive, the nose straight and the eyes candid. They were pleasant, friendly eyes, a warm brown with tints of gold; in colouring they matched her hair, which she wore short, and which had natural curls. Her complexion however left a margin for improvement. It was pale, and had a tendency to porousness that bothered her. She had taken advice about this and was using a recommended cream, but to the best of her observation its effect was largely moral. Still, it might have been worse. She had few lines over which to frown. Taking her head to foot, she was a woman likely to turn any man thoughtful. She was no longer a blushing maiden but she had achieved a piquant maturity, her body was full of wisdom, it held sophisticated promise. Had she really intended to retire it into the limbo of perpetual indifference?

'Damn it, Stella, put yourself to bed.'

She whisked on her cream with reproving vigour. While she did so she tried to recapture the stricken mood she had experienced earlier – she was deserving of reproach for her frivolous meditations.

With an effort she managed to make her last waking thought of Justin, she remembered him touching his hat from the other side of the barrier. The swine! He hadn't even had the guts to tell her. Along with his other iniquities, the rotten so-and-so was a coward.

9

On the very next day she ran into Keith again.

During the morning she had taken great pains to continue her programme, performing all the little rituals that led to her sitting down to her typewriter. In these there was nothing superstitious or intrinsically useful but they formed an established pattern at the summit of which she began to write. Like many authors Stella was lazy, and particularly so this morning. She felt a powerful disinclination to going down to the summerhouse. She noticed a tendency to sit thinking, to muse on anything that came to mind. She fought it bravely; she went on with her preparation. She liked to consider herself a reliable author.

But having got to her typewriter she found her efforts had been in vain and that no amount of brute will-power would take the place of inspiration. She finished a sentence which had been broken off at the bottom of the last sheet, but then she simply sat and stared at the blank paper beneath it. The weather, most unfortunately, continued to be fine. Every water-lily was out on her private sheet of water. Sails chased each other beyond the reed islands, swallows came and went in the boathouse, she could hear the chittering of countless sedge-warblers and the distant throb of passing engines. It was neither the day nor the place for writing; the mood engendered was of languorous calm. One felt that the only business of life was to lounge and to soak up the sensuous beauty.

So she had given it up and gone to the boathouse, suddenly remembering the dinghy that Simon had left there. It was a sturdy-looking clinker-built craft and she fetched it out in some eagerness. Did she remember how things went? It was some years since she had sailed a dinghy. She puzzled a little over the sail, but eventually got it set up fair. She had to paddle away from the staithe because the alders blanketed the wind, but soon her tan sail caught a puff and the willing dinghy began to travel. She felt a thrill of pure pleasure – this was better than pounding a typewriter! She put in a few quite needless tacks, just to get the feel of the little boat. Then she passed close to the houseboat, where the fisherman looked out and waved, and gybed rather breathlessly to point her bows towards the Broad.

The Broad was larger than she had supposed. Its shape was irregular and it was bounded by endless reed-swamp, forming innumerable bays and inlets and giving glimpses of secret lagoons beyond. It was divided almost in two by a large island and red and black posts marked the sailing channels, but the dinghy was not confined by these and Stella was free to go where she would. On a soldier's wind she sped up the Broad among the yachts and burbling motor cruisers, then turned out of the busy channels to explore the quieter margins. The reed-swamp was delectable; there one could penetrate hidden pools and tiny creeks, and everywhere floated the starry white lilies along with the scented yellow 'brandy-bottles'. At length she chose a spot and moored. She dropped the sail and lit a cigarette. She couldn't remember the last time when a cigarette had tasted so sweet. She felt a dreamy sense of peace, of unconcern and complacency, as though the world and all her troubles had slipped that moment out of the reckoning. She smoked her cigarette and didn't give a damn.

Half an hour later she became aware of Keith. He was sailing a National Twelve dressed in smart new terylene sails. She saw it turn in a flutter at the top of the Broad and instantly recognized the helmsman – and was a little appalled to discover that the recognition gave her pleasure. But hadn't she settled all that last night, deciding to be firm and only amused. She made a hasty review of her feelings . . . yes, she *was* only amused by Keith! At the same time she had to admit an interest, Keith was a case, and she wanted to study him: it would need careful handling, perhaps, but there could be no harm in a few soulful exchanges. She stood up, she waved to him. Keith saw her and put over his helm. The National wove towards her mooring in a series of dashing little tacks, then slid fastidiously through the reeds and brought up short beside the dinghy. He reached over and took hold of her gunnel.

'I wondered . . . I noticed the dinghy was out.'

'You went down to the summerhouse, did you?'

'Yes, I thought you might like a trip.'

'I did. But I didn't wait to be asked.'

She smiled warmly into his earnest eyes. The lamb, he'd devised an excuse to visit her! And he'd squandered a clean shirt and pressed his shorts, and combed a severe parting into his hair.

'You'd better drop your sails, hadn't you? They'll drag us both off the mooring.'

He flushed as though she had made a daring suggestion.

'Yes, I'd better . . . I'll tie up to yours.'

'It's very pleasant moored here. It's curious, but people don't seem to stray much from the channel.'

He took in sail with a clumsy briskness. He seemed far too large for the delicate National. Under the parade of lighting another cigarette, Stella coolly appraised him. At thirty-three, she was not a woman lacking in experience. Her curiosity had provoked her into more than one affair. She had embarked on them critically and with affection rather than passion; it had been reserved for Justin to touch her heart – and to fob her off with a salute. She knew something about men and she was not ashamed of her knowledge. She had taken pleasure in their attentions and she was not ashamed of that. And she knew now, eyeing Keith, that she would find him intriguing to love, and that his shamefaced virginity made no small part of his attraction. It was a novelty that piqued her. She had never had a student lover.

'There . . . that's about it. I don't think we shall rub.'

'You had better come into my dinghy. You look cramped over there.'

'Well, if you like . . .'

'Then we'll bask and have a chat. You can tell me about yourself, and perhaps recite some of your poetry.'

She thought he would have them both in, he was so awkward in changing boats; their two masts waved drunkenly and the National shipped water. She made use of the opportunity to take him by the hand, then sat him firmly on the floorboards by her seat.

'Do you smoke, by the way?'

'No. No thanks.'

'You will never make a poet. You should buy yourself a pipe.'

'I don't think I'd like it.'

'You are at the experiencing age. It's your business to try everything that offers, my lad.'

He crossed his long legs and tried to look at his ease, but his situation on the floorboards was neither dignified nor comfortable. The seat on which Stella perched was pressing into the small of his back and he had to screw his head round when he wanted to speak to her. She was well aware of his discomfort. She smoked her cigarette placidly. At her feet was where he belonged and where she intended he should be. She carelessly flicked away some ash, brushing his shoulder as she did so. She felt a sense of well-being, of an honest woman aboon her might.

'How long have you been down here?'

'Oh, on Tuesday. I came straight from Cambridge.'

He made an effort to twist his body so that he could remain looking up at her.

'When do you see your people?'

'People? Well, there's only grandfather. My father was killed, you know. He was in that train crash at Glasgow.'

'I'm sorry. I didn't know.'

'That's all right. We weren't very . . . close. And then there's my mother. I've never met her. She was divorced soon after I was born.'

'I've put my foot in it, haven't I?'

'But it doesn't matter. I want you to know.'

She laughed, but rather wryly. The poor dear soul! So he was quite alone. He not only looked but he was bereft, there was only a grandfather and Uncle Simon. She was going to have something to shoulder if she took up with Master Keith.

'So you live with your grandfather, do you?'

'Yes. He's interested in my career. I'm supposed to go into the family firm – that's Lea-Stephens Engineering. I'm the only one left to go in, so there isn't much I can do about it. But I loathe the business really. I think I'll probably be a flop.'

'Why do you think that?'

'Oh, I don't know. I just feel it. I'm not a bit like my father, I don't take much to engineering. I didn't want to take physics. I would have liked an arts degree. I shall scrape through it somehow, but that's about all.'

'What did you want to do, then?'

'I don't know.' He looked dreamy. 'That's been the whole trouble, I didn't have an alternative.'

'You just want to be a poet?'

'No. Definitely not.' He shook his head. 'It's got no meaning any longer. One might as well want to be a dodo.'

She glanced at him, surprised. 'You're a fine one to talk!'

'But it's true,' he replied earnestly. 'Didn't you tell me so yourself? It's elementary, one grows out of it. I've been thinking about what you said. Poetry doesn't mean anything any longer. We've got past it. It's too naïve.'

'I didn't go so far as that.'

'No, but it's true, and I've known it, really. It never occurred to me to set up as a poet. But I didn't know why, until you told me.'

She drew hard on her cigarette and eyed him a little askance. He was a more complicated person than Stella had taken him for. She didn't know why, but she had been inclined to think of him as a silly young man. Quite obviously he wasn't, he had a brain. She felt the tiniest bit aggrieved.

'Perhaps you want to write novels, then?'

'I don't think I could do that.'

'It's easy. You just sit and you write and write and write.'

'It can't be as easy as all that.' He gave her a shy little smile. 'Besides, I'm only twenty, you know. I haven't got much material.'

'There's a stack of it at Lazy Waters.'

'Oh yes, but I couldn't use it.'

'Take Dawn Le Fay, for instance.'

'She's odd. She's rather funny.'

'She's got a thing for you.'

He moved uneasily and turned away from her. 'I don't know . . . she's a peculiar girl. She isn't serious, it's just a game.'

'She's beautiful.'

'Oh yes . . . her looks.'

'Her figure too.'

'Yes, she's got a figure . . .'

'Then why not play with her, for what it's worth. Some men would give their eyes for the chance.'

He hung his head over her knees, revealing a soft, downy nape, but though his face was turned from her he couldn't conceal a hot flush. Stella smiled to herself. He wasn't so complex, really. He was just a defenceless little boy whose emotions led him by the nose. She thought it would be rather nice to slip her arm around his shoulder, to ruffle the fine young hair which he had taken such pains with.

'She would probably give you a good time.'

'Yes . . .'

'You like her style, don't you? She mightn't be an intellectual, but she isn't stupid either. I think you'd get on well together.' (You bloody liar, Stella.) 'And there's material for a novel, just waiting for you to pick it up.'

'But I don't want to write a novel!'

'It's material, all the same.'

'Please, I don't want you to think –'

'You wouldn't be scared by a chit like that?'

Now she did yield to the temptation to rest her arm on his shoulders, lightly, compassionately, with a sister-like touch. His reaction surprised her. He clasped her passionately by the waist. He buried his face in her bosom and held it there, shuddering.

'Steady on, my lad!'

This was faster than she expected. She looked around hastily to make certain that their concealment was effective. Then she shifted herself to give a more comfortable position, gently removed one of his arms and placed her hand on his head. Some soulful exchanges, indeed! He'd got the makings of a wolf.

'This isn't the time and place, you know.'

'Stella –'

'You had better take things easy.'

'Stella, I've got to tell you –!'

'You're a pet lamb, and you're rather wicked.'

He moaned and went on pressing his face to her. She could feel the heat of his cheeks. She took charge of a hand which had fallen on her knee, but she didn't think it entirely necessary to remove it. His lips sought her hotly through her thin blouse and she allowed herself a moment of luxurious sensation.

'That's enough, my pet. Now you're going to behave.'

She took him briskly by the hair and drew his head away from her. His smoky, sultry eyes had a strangely broken look, like the eyes of an animal when it feels a fatal wound. He remained quite still, staring up at her, his lips slightly parted. She felt a strong impulse to kiss him but she countered it with a stronger one.

'You're not the angel you look, are you?'

'Stella . . . you understand . . .'

'I understand that we're sitting in a dinghy, and that passers-by are likely to see us.'

'I love you, Stella!'

'You're an idiot, Keith.'

'I do . . . I love you. You must believe me.'

'You'd do better to stick with Dawn.'

'Dawn! She's nothing. She's just a girl.'

'She's nearer your age than I am, and she doesn't lack the inclination.'

'But she's a girl, that's the point. Stella, you must see it . . . I love you. It just happened. I can't help it. I saw you, and I knew . . .'

'I'm too old for you, my pet.'

'No! It's just because of that . . .'

'Yes I am. It wouldn't be fair to you.'

'But I don't care. I love you!'

This time he burrowed his face in her lap, and she let it stay there, still grasping his hair. She was more than a little startled by the vehemence of his passion, and perhaps even more by his clear-sighted intuition. He was plainly aware of what Stella represented. She was a sophisticated woman, and as such he was seeking her. He had understood with sure instinct what her brain had tardily surmised, that it was in a relationship such as this that he could find emotional salvation. Dawn, poor Dawn, she was only a girl; it was Dawn, not he, who was too young.

'You really are a poppet, my dear.'

'Stella . . .'

'I probably ought to spank you.' She stroked the soft hair

which she found so attractive and didn't interfere when he pressed kisses on her.

'You're only a boy, you know that, don't you?'

'I love you Stella. I need you. I need you.'

'To me you're just a boy.'

'I'll be anything, Stella . . .'

'An idiotic boy who should do what he's told.'

'I will, I promise.'

'Then you had better begin now. Because it's lunchtime, my lad, and I don't like to be late for meals.'

'But Stella –'

'No buts – you'll do just as you're told. So break up the party and hop out of my boat.'

She was inflexible; and very reluctantly, he obeyed her command. She made him set out before her and watched him safely down the Broad. But when he was safely out of earshot she burst into uncontrollable laughter, certainly the first time she had done that since she'd read the announcement in the *Telegraph*.

10

And the more she thought about what had happened the more Stella felt the inclination to laugh: it was so ridiculous, so sudden, and was having such an absurd effect on her. Less than twenty-four hours had passed since she had first met Keith, and yet during that time her whole outlook had taken a somersault. Quite frankly the effect was disproportionate to the cause. Keith was amusing, he was unexpected, she felt a qualified interest in him; but nothing could hide the fact that at first she had scarcely noticed him. And yet the cause had produced the effect: at lunchtime today she was a different person. She kept thinking of Keith, and giggling. She didn't think of Justin at all.

When she had finished her lunch and tidied up she went to sit on the bench in the garden. She had ceased to have any idea of working; she had a premonition that novel was about to slide into oblivion. It was the greatest shame, of course, after the unhappy week she had spent on it, but it was a novel of mood, and she'd lost the mood, so it was really pointless to grind away at it. Meanwhile, she had thinking to do and, putting up her legs, she gave it her attention.

First, Simon: could the brute have foreseen that something like this was going to happen? She remembered his lecture. It seemed very odd that he should discuss with her the logic of affairs, and then five minutes later produce Keith from up his sleeve. It had the appearance of contrivance, of astute stage-management, and she wouldn't put it past Simon to play such a trick. An amoral person himself he would see in it nothing reprehensible: on the contrary, he would probably view it as a kindly little gesture. And he could have a deeper motive, too. She suspected he was interested in Dawn. If that were the case, then it would be to his interest to have Keith occupied elsewhere. Yes, her suspicions of Simon were fair, he had been the tiniest little bit two-faced. She didn't blame him, but she didn't like it – damn it, he might have come out in the open!

But then she smiled at her indignation because, after all, how could Simon have been open with her? In her present mood he might have been, but yesterday had been different. She forgave him; she saw that he was only being tactful. He had jogged her attention, that was all, and she couldn't quarrel with him for doing that. He had wished Keith on her without pain, and now it was up to Stella whether Keith was one of *her* acceptances.

Well, she hadn't fallen for Keith, and she had too much common sense to suppose that he was really in love with her. He thought he was, she didn't doubt; his protestations were sincere. In a whirlpool of anxious emotions he had equated his need for her with love. But it wasn't love at all: it was an alarmed and fearful instinct. He wanted the knowledge of her person and the reassurance of her consent, along with the relief of having his own desire acknowledged and accepted. He was a neophyte facing a mystery and she the priestess who could unfold it, she was mature in the ways of love. In every sense she would be his mistress.

She sighed a little complacently at the end of this analysis, for it wasn't unpleasing to feel that she was such an important person to him. To be the focus of so much ardour at the age of thirty-two was a compliment to her attraction that was worth lingering over. About Keith however there could be no illusions, and she was glad that she could view the young man objectively. She wasn't even certain if she particularly liked him; beneath his romanticism she suspected there lay much that was commonplace. No: if she accepted Keith – and here Stella looked keenly into her soul – it would be mostly because she was rather attracted to the poor lamb physically. She had a yearning to take unto herself all his blind, tremulous youth, to deflower him with her body, to crop the bloom of his callowness. Having admitted this she reviewed it with meticulous care. It was true: she had felt the pang of it when he was with her that morning. And he was willing – but was it fair? That was the truly critical question. As she turned it over she frowned, and dug her thumbnail into the bench.

Then suddenly she realised that she wasn't alone, and the circumstances gave her a start. Standing near her, cap in hand, was the man who had wanted to do her garden. He must have approached very silently because she hadn't heard a sound, and now his thin-lipped mouth grinned at her, obviously in triumph at her surprise.

'Didn't mean to scare you, missus.'

She put down her legs and smoothed her skirt. He wasn't elderly by any means, and she noticed now that he had a roving eye. She gave him a stare that was intended to quell him.

'I don't remember hearing you knock.'

'That's all right, missus, I didn't knock. Thought I might find you sitting out here.'

'What do you want?'

'Well, I just came by. You were going to consider me, if you remember. I've always seen to the garden here – once or twice a week, that's the regular thing.'

She got up. She wasn't sure that she liked his familiar grin, while he had an attitude about him of being very much at home. He was a hard-framed, wiry-haired man with narrow, pinched and weathered features, and his eyes, as well as roving, had a quirk of mockery in them.

'I still think you might have knocked.'

'Well, you know, I'm not used to your ways.'

'They are much the same as other people's.'

He smirked as though she had said something witty.

'I used to come looking for the other lady, and it's hard to break a habit. Very fond of the garden, she was, she was always lying about on a rug. She never minded me a bit. Aren't you an actress sort-of lady?'

'No, I'm not.'

'But that's all right, though.'

'I'm glad you think so.'

'Ah. You're all right.'

Stella tried another stare but found it quite without effect. The fellow, Sam, she remembered his name was, seemed armed against reproofs of that kind. She came to the point.

'I shan't need your services.'

'Ay?' It was his turn to be surprised. 'But missus, I always see to the garden. I know how things are run around here.'

'I'm sorry. I'm making other arrangements.'

He didn't seem able to take it in. He stood staring, his mouth open, the coarse skin wrinkling on his forehead.

'But missus, look you here! I'm a bloke you can trust, just ask Mr Simon. You needn't worry about me. I'm as quiet as the grave when it comes to that sort of thing.'

'Exactly what do you mean?' She felt a pinprick of apprehension – could this lout have been a witness to what passed that morning in the dinghy? Seeing that his words had made an impression, he drew closer, at the same time sinking his voice confidentially.

'We all know Mr Simon, don't we? One of the lads, he is! And I like his taste too, I didn't quarrel with it last time. Of course, I know my place, missus. I'm the bloke that does the garden. But

I'm around, don't you worry. And I never breathe a word.'

With the leer that accompanied the words his meaning was now plain enough, and Stella started back from him in angry revulsion. She was shocked. Surely she didn't look like a woman of that sort? Her hand itched, and she barely refrained from striking him across the face.

'Get off these premises!'

His leer vanished. 'Now missus, don't get upshus –'

'Get off these premises, do you hear?'

'I'll go when I'm fit.'

'You'll go now, or I'll ring the police.'

'I'll go when I'm fit, not when you order me!'

There was a battle of eyes between them but finally Stella's anger won it. He shuffled, he dragged on his cap, but in the end he dropped his gaze.

'But don't you go thinking –'

'That's enough. Get out of here.'

'You're making a big mistake, missus.'

'Just get out. And don't dare come back.'

He went, though not without several meaningful and insolent glances. She felt hot and was quivering with the intensity of her anger. The foul beast, to come making such overtures to her – so familiar and insinuating! She couldn't get over the insult of it. And Simon: it was Simon who had let her in for this scene. In a moment of angry insight she understood the whole business. He had bought the cottage for one of his women – that accounted for the expense of it – he had lodged a real floozie in it, one he was ashamed to have up at the house. And Stella, the innocent, had inherited the woman's reputation. All over the village, very probably, she was being regarded as a tart. In a seething rage she went indoors and snatched up the phone – she was going to let Simon know just what she thought about it.

'Stella darling, is it?' Dawn's sugary tones greeted her.

'I want to have a word with Simon.'

'That's a pity darling. He's out.'

'Where's he gone?'

'I wouldn't know darling. They went off in the launch. I'm

the only one who stopped. Oh, and Keith. But he's disappeared.'

'That was thoughtless of him, darling.'

Stella hung up with a bang. And swore.

11

As was usual with Stella's rages this one quickly blew itself out,
so that before long she was grinning at what had just happened.
She had a lively sense of the ridiculous both in herself and in
others and she could rarely sustain a feeling of being injured for
long. She was tickled now to imagine her would-be gardener's
disappointment. The silly idiot had been so confident that he
would be welcomed with open arms. She remembered his
incredulity, his note of rightful indignation: it was too absurd.
She wondered if the fellow wasn't perhaps weak-minded. But
she was somewhat less inclined to be charitable towards Simon.
This was the second time she had caught him out in a deception
towards herself. He might have warned her about the cottage,
that was the least he should have done; she didn't think it would
have put her off, but she would have been more on her guard
with the locals.

Some resentment remained, and she stuck to her resolve to
have the matter out with Simon. He would most likely be back
for tea and she had a standing invitation, so she locked the door
of the cottage and set off for Lazy Waters. When she arrived
Dawn was still the only person there. She was lying decora-
tively sunbathing on a towel spread on the lawn. The two parts
of a bikini lay beside her and also a large box of chocolates; she
peered up at Stella through outsize sunglasses, then gestured
towards the chocolates.

'Darling, I've been so bored today.'

Stella sighed to herself but took a seat in a deck-chair. In a

moment of irritation she thought that Dawn looked almost
obscene: the starlet's body was completely depilated and she
had nipples as broad as crown pieces.

'Didn't Keith come back, darling?'

'No darling. Have you seen him?' Dawn raised her sunglasses and her blue eyes sparkled with a touch of animosity.
'He's a strange boy, isn't he? He doesn't seem to have any interests. Or I didn't think he had. He's unbelievably shy.'

'He's a poet or something, darling.'

'Well I don't think it's healthy. He's too young for it, anyway.
Aren't you a poet, darling?'

Stella shrugged carelessly and reached for a chocolate. Dawn
watched her moodily. She fumbled in the box. She chewed
chocolates languidly and with an introspective greed. ('My girl,
just you wait. Just you wait till you're thirty.')

'Have you known Simon long darling?'

'No, darling. Have you?'

Dawn undulated gently. 'Yes darling. He's nice. I've known
him almost two years. I think Glynda's very lucky. I think she's
jealous of you darling.'

'She has no reason to be, darling.'

'No darling, I'm sure of it. Actually Simon never mentioned
you before you turned up here. But she's jealous of Jill too, and
that's perfectly fantastic. She must know that Jill is les, because
it stands out a mile.'

'Is she jealous of you, darling?'

'But darling, of course. She was terribly awkward about my
coming here. I haven't the slightest idea why Simon took up
with her. She hasn't any talent. Or none that anyone has
noticed.'

'Perhaps she makes a change, darling.'

Dawn nodded her head seriously. 'Men can be odd darling,
that's one thing a girl learns. But Simon is very sweet, he does
his best to be nice to her. You'd really be surprised to know the
pains he goes to.'

Stella supressed a smile; she thought she had an idea. She felt
certain now of why Dawn was laying for Keith. The poor

52

cherub was a sacrifice to keep Glynda docile, and it was Simon who had indicated this prudent diversion.

'Simon is *very* sweet.'

Dawn eyed her suspiciously. 'Of course, you have to know him darling. Simon is like that to everyone. I was the tiniest bit surprised when I heard you'd got the cottage, but then it's different, this year. Or is it I wonder?'

'It's different, darling.'

'Yes. I thought it must be. You're not the least bit like Vanessa, are you?'

'I didn't know Vanessa.'

'Vanessa was a bitch darling. He had to keep her tucked away because his father sometimes stays here.'

Dawn reached for a fresh chocolate and sank her teeth in it with relish. Stella couldn't forbear a glance at the starlet's smooth stomach. At the moment it was flattish with the barest twirl of a navel, but given a month or so of this treatment Dawn would really be having worries. It was a satisfying thought. Stella lit a cigarette.

'Have you met Simon's father darling?'

'No.' Stella exhaled.

'He's quite a nice old boy. I didn't find him a bit alarming. Of course I dressed the part darling, Simon told me what was expected. Rather drab you know, just a touch of the vicar's daughter.'

'You were staying here with him?'

'Darling don't be absurd. Simon took me to supper with him, and Woody, and Jill. It was during the *Girl*. Simon's father came to vet it. Simon cued us all in and we put on the act of our tiny lives. Improvisation too darling. We were really quite something.'

'And Simon's father was impressed?'

'Oh yes. He lapped it up. It was after the row about Vanessa, so it was rather important to Simon.'

'I hadn't heard about the row.'

'No darling. But there was one. Simon's father is hung up about sex. He's got his knife into actresses.'

Stella's complacency increased as she meditated this tit-bit. It was cheering to know that Simon had his troubles with the lurid Vanessa. She felt a little less sour towards him, he had already received his punishment. It might even be that in letting her the cottage he was making a gesture of contrition. It wasn't probable, perhaps, but she'd give him the benefit of the doubt.

'Keith is very unlike his uncle, isn't he?'

'Yes he is.' Dawn was undulating again. She had a suggestive, serpent-like motion that seemed to remember an ecstatic embrace. No doubt she had learned it at RADA or somewhere. 'Actually, I thought you were getting on rather well with him.'

'Two poets, darling. We had things to talk about.'

'Poetry must be a fascinating subject darling.'

'It passes the time, darling. It isn't so dull.'

'Yes. I could see that.' Dawn's action was jerkier. 'In fact I thought Keith was finding it quite exciting. I thought it was a pity darling. He's very young, isn't he? I'm rather young myself and he isn't quite as old as me.'

'Poets are usually young, darling.'

'Yes darling. Usually. And he's rather silly. He doesn't know what he wants.'

'It is just conceivable, darling, that you don't understand him.'

'Quite darling. Though I think I may be the proper one to try.'

Dawn flashed her eyes at Stella then let the sunglasses sink over them. She lay still with an expression of delicious repose on her face. She parted her knees very slightly and flexed her none-too-clean toes.

'Darling,' she said, 'I'm so unutterably bored.'

12

Stella went down to the river where she could sit watching the boats, but she didn't have long to wait before the launch returned. The launch had a throbbing diesel engine which one could identify at some distance, so that she was aware of its approach before it actually left the Broad. It was an impressive, slipper-sterned vessel built of lustrous red mahogany, with a chromium-plated stemplate and a battery of chromium-plated lamps. From a raked pennant-mast flew Simon's personal burgee, while over the streamlined stern fluttered a big red ensign. Simon was at the helm himself; he was wearing a red blazer and a yachting cap. He lifted the latter and gave it a wave when he caught sight of Stella. Glynda, who was also wearing a bikini (who was trying to upstage whom?), sat beside him, while the others lounged among cushions in the back. Simon brought the launch to the quay with a prettily calculated manoeuvre, gave a short burst of reverse and touched fenders to the heading.

'Surprise, my dear.'

His smile was all ready for her. He handed her the bow painter and contrived to press her hand while doing so. His eyes had been anxious but her responding smile cleared them. Glynda watched them bitchily; she had a hand on Simon's arm.

'I was wondering if we would have the pleasure of seeing you today.'

'Thank you, Simon. I felt I would like some company.'

'Keith mentioned at lunch that he'd met you on the Broad. If I were you I would drop working – there are so many better things to do.'

'You may be right. Anyway, I've stopped working.'

He seemed genuinely pleased that Stella had returned so soon to Lazy Waters, and made a fuss of her that did nothing to placate the sullen Glynda. She stuck by Simon like his shadow, her wide mouth shut tight. It occurred to Stella that the actress might be close to having a part found for her. Woody ambled across to Stella.

'Should have joined us for the trip, girlo. Sweet parts these are, just one long loaf.'

'Did you ever need an excuse, Woody?'

His big face grinned down at her. She wondered if it were possible to guess what went on in Woody's head.

'Seen any more of the kid, girlo?'

'Not since this morning. Should I have done?'

'Thought I saw him in the sailboat in the offing of your spread.'

Stella swore to herself. Damn the lovelorn little idiot! 'I'm told it's a good spot for fishing,' she said.

'Yeah.' Woody didn't look either convinced or unconvinced, he just continued to grin in his outsize way. Stella hesitated for a moment but then decided to let it lie. Woody could think what he liked: who the hell was Woody anyway?

'You should try fishing yourself. I should have thought it would have suited you.'

'Too true it would, girlo. But I'd have to dig the bait.'

'You buy it, Woody.'

'Then I'd have to hook it on.'

'You could bribe the gardener.'

'Break it down! I might happen to catch something.'

Stella wasn't sure why the incident gave her an unpleasant feeling and she was silent as she accompanied the party up the lawn. She kept repeating to herself: What does it matter? Why should I care? – but could think of no satisfactory answer to either question. It was none of their business if she played around with Keith. If they knew, they would think it nothing out of the ordinary. Yet she didn't want them to know, she felt a reluctance that she couldn't account for; she felt annoyed with herself and somehow angry with Keith. She would have to instil some discretion into him if the relationship was to develop.

Keith didn't come in for tea, and for this Stella was thankful. The meal was taken outdoors on a table under one of the tall willows. Its feathery leaves were ruffled by breeze, admitting sun in little bursts, and from where they sat it was still possible to watch the idle passing of boats. When tea was over, both Glynda and Dawn felt a sudden need for a change of raiment; and Stella seized the opportunity to get Simon on his own.

'I would like to look at your boats, Simon.'

Simon was on his feet at once. Nobody who wanted to admire his possessions was likely to meet with reluctance from him. He led her across to the boathouse and held the door for her to go through. Inside half a dozen fine craft lay moored along the stagings for her inspection.

'An evening's row or a fortnight's cruise?'

'Just a chat, if you don't mind, Simon.'

He raised his eyebrows enquiringly, then pointed to a motor-cruiser.

'*Puma* will be the most comfortable. I had her lounge refitted in the spring.'

They went on board and down steps into a cabin furnished with capacious settee-berths. It smelled of fresh varnish and new fabrics and one trod on spongy carpet. Before he sat down, Simon couldn't help prowling round it and demonstrating its several conveniences.

'And now, my dear, what can this very serious chat be about?'

Stella looked at him pointedly. 'It's about the cottage, that's what.'

'The cottage?' He sounded surprised. 'But I thought you were settling in so well.'

'I thought so too. But I find it has a reputation.'

'Oho.' Simon placed a comfortable arm around her shoulder; he had a way of doing this that was entirely inoffensive. 'I didn't think that would give you any trouble.'

'I'm not sure I altogether believe you, Simon.'

57

'My dear! But truthfully, I thought your character was safe enough.'

'So did I till this afternoon. But now I'm certain it's mud in Alderford.'

She told him about Sam Fulcher. Simon heard her out gravely. She wondered if he had known about Vanessa and the gardener, but, if he hadn't, he gave no sign of surprise. When she had finished he sighed gently.

'It's a sordid story, isn't it?'

'Well Simon, I don't propose to set up as judge.'

'Oh but it is, my dear. I was a damned fool over Vanessa. She was mire for me to roll in – I'm a masochist at times – and roll in it I did. I have the grace to be ashamed.'

'And the cottage – that was laid on for her?'

'Something like that, I have to admit. My father comes down here during the summer, and I have to try not to offend him. He belongs to the pre-permissive generation and now I'm his only son, so when he stays here I clear the decks. That was the purpose of the cottage.'

'But he was bound to find out sooner or later.'

Simon gave her a quick look. 'My dear, I suspect that you've been raking up gossip.'

'I didn't need to rake it up. I had only to sit beside Dawn.'

'Ah yes. Dear Dawn.'

'You have to allow that I would be interested.'

Simon sighed again and offered her his cigarette-case. They lit cigarettes and blew smoke into the expensive cabin. He had the smallest of frowns on his well-proportioned brow and she had the feeling, as once before, that he was trying to find words for something difficult to say. But in the end he merely shrugged and flicked cigarette ash.

'Life is a wretchedly complicated business, though in our trade I suppose we should be thankful for that. I'm fond of my father in my own perverse way. He needs handling, that's all. He has a weakness for high principles.'

'I heard that you'd had a row, but that you had made it up afterwards.'

'Ye-es.' For some reason Simon looked relieved.

'And now I suppose the cottage has lost the best part of its usefulness.'

He gave her his most charming smile. 'Not as long as you are my tenant, my dear.'

'All the same, you might pass it around that I'm not your latest.'

'I'll speak to Fulcher, of course.'

'You can tell him that I'm a nun.'

Stella smoked on more contentedly. She thought she was right in liking Simon. He had his faults, and they were many, but one could depend on his good will. He was kindly, and frank. You didn't have to choose words with him. In a way he was stimulating, and he was always fun to be with.

'By the way, my dear.'

'Yes, Simon?'

'With regard to Dawn. Whether it's true or not, she thinks you've spoiled her pitch with Keith.'

'Should I worry about that?'

'Not too terribly you shouldn't. Only Dawn is a spiteful kitten, so I thought I had better warn you.'

'She gave me the same impression.' Stella was surprised by her complacence. With Simon, she found, she could discuss the matter without distress.

'I think Dawn rather had the impression that Keith was invited for her benefit, and in a way he was. I thought they might pair-off usefully.'

'Usefully, yes.' Stella queried him with a look. So Simon had engineered this balance of interest from the beginning. In a moment he would probably hint to her to soft-pedal with Keith – his falling for her had upset the delicate equation at Lazy Waters.

'Of course it doesn't matter, my dear, and I'm not pretending it does. It's up to Keith. He's the heir to the self-will of the Lea-Stephens. Dawn can divert herself elsewhere, Jeff is falling over his feet for her. And I'm not sure that Dawn would be the best thing for Keith anyway.'

A different turn to the plot! Stella had forgotten about Jeff. But now she could easily see how he might come into the reckoning.

'As you say, it's up to Keith.'

'And up to you, I rather imagine.'

'You're being a little premature, Simon.'

'My dear, you only have to snap your fingers. Keith has got the complaint badly, you know that as well as I. He has taste, I will say that for him. I wish I had met you when I was his age.'

'That's an Irish sort of compliment.'

Simon kissed her with gentle appreciation. 'You know what I mean. You'd be a heaven-send to him. He would remember you all the rest of his life. And I wish I'd met a woman like you instead of the little tart I took up with.'

'You would be a better man, no doubt.'

'Seriously, yes. May I kiss you again?'

'How long does Glynda take to dress?'

'Half an hour, my dear.'

'Then you'd better be quick.'

13

Keith put in an appearance in time for supper, and annoyed Stella by gazing at her with soulful, reproaching eyes. If anyone had been in doubt before, she thought, they must know now that the young man was infatuated with her. She snubbed him without mercy, and took a sadistic pleasure in it. After supper she was at pains to join the conversation of the others. She had the pleasure of seeing him retire into self-banishment with a book, and of eventually disappearing from the company altogether. She felt cruelly satisfied with what she had done and she pressed her triumph by twitting Woody.

But she was quickly to learn that Keith meant to have the last word. When, at eleven, she returned to the cottage, she found him there waiting in the garden. She had refused a lift from

Simon and had walked home deep in her musings, and when she caught sight of Keith it gave her quite a shock.

'You! What do you mean by coming here to the cottage?'

He was standing as still as a post by the bench under the apple-tree. To the lingering twilight the stars were adding a pale radiance, so that he really did have a ghostly appearance against the dark mass of the tree.

'Stella.'

She went over to him. She was in a panic of anger. God, the place was rank enough already in the local nostrils. It wanted only Fulcher to come prying along the lane and she would be branded for ever in the annals of Alderford.

'Keith, just you listen to me. I won't have you coming here. Don't dare to do it again or I shall never forgive you.'

'But Stella, I had to come –'

'You're a stupid blundering idiot. You're a nitwit, Keith. Now for heaven's sake go.'

His face was too pale for it to have been simply the starlight and his expression was pitiable: she could hear his teeth nittering. He put out a shaky hand, as though to placate her wrath. He looked as though a push would have been enough to send him toppling.

'I had to, Stella . . . you seemed angry . . .'

'Angry! My God! That's putting it mildly.'

'But why? What have I done?'

'You've come here, you blithering goose.'

'No, but before that –'

'Before that you were being a fool.'

He rocked, and made another placating motion with his hand, and this time she felt a little surge of pity for him. He was genuinely in a bad way, the helpless chump that he was. He had worked himself up so far that he was likely to go off in a faint.

'Sit down then, blast you.'

'But Stella, tell me –'

'Sit down and stop waving about like a reed.'

He sat down heavily, and after a moment Stella sat herself decorously beside him.

61

'Now I'm going to tell you something, and you'll remember it, my lad. I don't care what notions you've got stuffed in that woolly head of yours. There's a quality called discretion. It means exactly what it says. And you'd better know right away that I value it very highly.'

'But I haven't breathed a word, Stella –'

'It isn't necessary to breathe words. You've only to look like a dying duck and you've told the whole world. There's a lot of gush talked about love, my sweeting, but take a tip from your Aunty Stella. All the world hates a lover, and that's the first lesson in the business.'

'Stella, I didn't know . . .'

She let him lean against her with his arm half round her waist. The shock of finding him there was subsiding and with it the biting edge of her indignation. After all, it was a very secluded cottage, and on a by-road but little frequented. She had met not a soul on her walk from Lazy Waters, and the odds were high against anyone passing that way so late. She needn't have been so sharp with him perhaps, or so extinguishingly crushing. She kissed him on the forehead.

'I'm sorry, my pet, but honestly you must learn not to be so obvious. It's in bad taste, for one thing. It embarrasses other people. Love is a very excluding emotion and not to be exhibited in public. People who do it are either clowns or experiencing a sense of inadequacy, and you should avoid being the one and tackle the other with more intelligence.'

'It's so difficult, Stella.'

'It's a terribly difficult subject.'

'I just can't help feeling the way I do.'

'It's a phase, and I promise you it won't last for ever. So don't let it fool you. Try to see it with detachment.'

He drew a deep breath and laid his head on her shoulder. 'I think I could. I think . . . if only . . .'

She nodded to herself. He could, if only she would accept him. It was an occasion when being an elder sister was not enough.

'Now you had better be getting back, before someone starts wondering.'

62

'They won't.' He snuggled up a little closer. 'They're used to me going off for a row or a swim.'

'Not at this hour they aren't.'

'Yes – I'm always doing it. I love swimming in the dark, I've been right up the Broad.'

Stella was incredulous. 'You mean you've swum up there?'

'Yes. I've often swum five miles, you know. And in the dark it's curious, it gives you peculiar feelings. You seem alone, miles away, as though you were out in space somewhere.'

'You're a strange boy, Keith.'

'Oh, other fellows do it too. There's a man in Kings who swam to Waterbeach one night.'

'Suppose you got cramp or something?'

'Yes, that's rather interesting. I've found out how to float while I relax and get rid of it.'

Stella shook her head, still a little unbelieving. She sensed suddenly the gulf that thirteen years opened between them. He was still at the stunt age, imperfectly aware of any limitation. He wanted an excess of experience. He hadn't begun to weigh the cost.

'Anyway, I think you had better be making tracks, my son.'

'No Stella, not yet. Don't send me away yet.'

'And unless I tell you, you're not to come to the cottage any more.'

'I won't, Stella, honestly. But you seemed so angry with me.'

She let him hold her closer and kiss her. Her resentment was now appeased. There was something romantic in the hour and the cool, stock-scented garden. Moths were buzzing about her honeysuckle and flitting across the lawn, and the soft, still air seemed to carry an indefinable promise.

'Tomorrow . . .'

Quarter of an hour had passed in a silent, passive embrace. He had kissed her several times and fearfully moved his hand over her hip.

'What about tomorrow, pet?'

'We could . . . well, go for a trip in the halfdecker.'

Stella thought about it. 'Yes. We could.'

63

'You'll come then?'

'If it's fine.'

He was silent again, slightly withdrawn. But then he kissed her with dangerous emphasis. She laughed and pressed his knee with her hand:

'But this time you're really going, young man.'

14

And the morrow was fine. When Stella woke sun was sparkling past her curtains, while the moving shadows of foliage cast upon them promised just the right amount of breeze. She took her bath, and dressed, and put her breakfast on a tray, and ate it sitting in the garden while she read her letters and the paper. Among the former was a characteristic and commonsensical letter from Jenny. She smiled over it, it seemed written for a different person than herself. She no longer needed admonishments to keep cheerful and to Try To Meet People, or moral reflections on the dangers of idleness. Dear Jenny! But what would she have thought of Stella now? Who had shrugged off her tragedy overnight and had taken up with a fresh fellow? She decided she better hadn't mention Keith when she replied to that letter; then she smiled over it again before folding it away in its envelope.

Keith had promised to have the halfdecker at the staithe by ten o'clock, so she waited until twenty-past before setting out to the summerhouse. As she went through the carrs she caught sight of a scandalised sail. Then Keith, who'd been sitting by it, sprang to his feet and came forward.

'I thought perhaps you'd changed your mind!'

She chuckled silently at his relieved expression. 'You said you would be here at about this time, didn't you?'

'At ten o'clock, actually. But I got here earlier.'

'I must have lingered too long over breakfast.'

Simon's halfdecker was a high sail number in the local

one-design class. A slim, white enamelled boat with a touch of tumblehome in her lines, she had a dark green cove line and varnished mahogany transom. Her name, *Lutestring*, was painted on the transom in a flowing shadowed script.

'Would you like to sail her?'

'Oh yes. If you think I'm up to it.'

Keith bustled about setting the jib and raising the tall gunter peak. He was wearing a navy shirt, navy slacks and suspiciously new Magisters, and looked altogether a thoroughly presentable young man. She noticed a picnic bag stowed forward, and a most unseamanlike collection of cushions. She took her seat at the helm.

'Where were you thinking of going?'

'I don't know . . . about the Broad. We can go anywhere you like.'

'Where does the river go from here, out of the top end of the Broad?'

'Oh, Staybridge and some other places.'

'Right. The next port is Staybridge.'

He looked a little solemn at this and she knew that it hadn't been in his programme, but he had given her the choice and he would have to abide by it. She drew her sheet and sent the halfdecker chuckling away from the staithe. Keith settled down with the jib and kept his eyes fixed ahead.

There was breeze to spare on the wide acres of the Broad, enough to lift up the polished blue bottom of the halfdecker. It was a close haul to the top end, a tight, surging passage, in which they outpaced a couple of cruising yachts and even left motor-cruisers standing. Yet Stella felt no sense of strain as she handled helm and sheet. Perfectly balanced, the halfdecker rose precisely up the wind. She resembled some marine Pegasus, gentle, obedient to command, fierce to devour the way before her and unbearably jealous of competitors. To be sailing her gave Stella a feeling of exquisite satisfaction. In a mysterious, glorious way she seemed to be poised between wind and water. She found the Broad all too short, it should have gone on into infinity, she wanted the land to pass away and the open sea to stretch before her. She thought she understood why people like Justin took to the ocean, why they devised their tiny vessels and turned their bows to mighty waters. To be sailing was a thirst which grew as it was quenched, and the best that one could do was to seize on a semblance of the infinite.

But the Broad came to an end, and a beat up to Staybridge succeeded it. Yet this too had a fascination in its demands on skill and judgement. The wind here was uncertain, being affected by low trees, and Stella's helmsmanship was quickly tested as they now sped, now drifted. On either hand stretched the lush fen with stands of reed and gnarled willows; meadowssweet grew rankly along the banks, together with loosestrife and orange balsam. In the end, Stella found that the river too was undesirably short, and they were gliding into Staybridge before she was ready to quit the sport.

It was a sunny, sleepy mooring beside some rusted brick malthouses, Staybridge being at the end of a dyke and remote from the main river. Keith took the warps ashore while Stella fondly coiled the sheet. She gave it a twist and a little pat: she felt she had earned her title to it.

'It's too early for lunch, isn't it?'

'Yes, I suppose it is.'

Her watch showed barely twelve o'clock; the journey had taken little over an hour. She sat and sunned herself on a cushion, a cigarette between her lips, her mind replete and slightly dreamy with the pleasure the sail had given her. Keith, at the other end of the boat, was less inclined to be restful. He was sitting doubled up as though his stomach ached and boredly massaging his ankles. He ought to smoke, she thought, now was the time for him to put on a pipe.

'Did you think I handled her all right?'

'Yes. I thought you did well.'

'It's quite a time since I did any sailing, so it wouldn't be surprising if I were rusty.'

'But you weren't, you handled her beautifully.'

'My overtaking needs brushing up.'

'Honestly, I thought it was good.'

66

'It was lousy. But thanks all the same.'

She smiled to herself at his dejected figure. Well: he would learn, in time. If he had wanted to force the pace he would have done better to have stuck to Dawn.

'Now that we've arrived, what sort of place is this Staybridge?'

'Oh, just one of those places. A big sort of village.'

'Then we may as well give it a look. I want to buy some cigarettes.'

He walked silently beside her off the quay and towards the village, his hands in his pockets and his head drooped forward. The way led by a water-meadow overhung by young willows, and crossed a single-line railway before joining the village street. It was a place of lazy charm. A huge, square, flint church-tower overlooked the ambling street, which boasted a miniature town hall, a fire-station, two banks and several shops with old-fashioned fronts. In addition it had a curiously relaxed atmosphere as though everyone, not merely the yachters, were on holiday; though its back was turned to the river, still it was penetrated by a river-influence.

After strolling the length of the street, Stella went to buy her cigarettes, leaving Keith lounging outside and still affecting to be bored. He had an unfortunate way of suggesting that he was above her mundane interests and was politely condescending to these foibles of his senior. It irritated Stella, and she deliberately lingered in the shop. If the kid couldn't be more gracious, then she would leave him to stew in his juice. She spent some more idle minutes in choosing a postcard for Jenny, and then tried every ballpen in the shop before making her selection. Coming out, she gave Keith a brilliant smile:

'So sorry to keep you hanging about.'

'I don't mind. I don't mind a bit.'

So she squandered another ten minutes in writing the postcard.

Their lunch consisted of chicken salad and an apple tart, washed down with canned beer. Stella had worked up a sailing appetite and she ate hers with relish. From their mooring there was plenty to watch in the shape of other craft, a yacht or two, dinghies, and a motor-wherry that nudged in beside the maltings. When she had finished the meal, Stella sighed; she felt that this was the life for her. It was a long way from Kensington, and she cared not if it were further.

'Where now, my lad?'

Keith was repacking the bag huffily. He seemed to have drifted as far away from her as the flat in town. His foolish small mouth was tucked up in a bundle, there was a flush on his cheek, and as he worked he kept his eye firmly averted from where she sat. The stupid young man! For after all, she had promised him nothing: to spend the day sailing had been the limit of her assent. Didn't he guess that it was up to him to provide a mood, an emotional springboard, and that without it the best-intentioned of women would remain cool? True, it was perhaps her business to teach him, but she needed straw for her bricks, and while he was being such an ass she felt the effort was really beyond her.

'Back again, I suppose. At least we'll have the wind with us.'

'We passed two turnings coming up. Wouldn't they be worth exploring?'

He was silent for a moment as he buckled the straps of the bag, then he replied, carefully neutral, 'They go to Southery and Hunsett Bridge.'

'Well, and what are they like?'

'Oh, up Hunsett way it's shoaly.'

'And Southery?'

'It's supposed to be a Broad, but it's all grown up with reeds and stuff. Then there's a staithe at the end, and a guesthouse. There's nothing else.'

'All the same it sounds pleasant.'

'There's better sailing on the Broad.'

'Never mind, we have plenty of time. I think I'd like to go to Southery.'

She couldn't help it, there was a devil in her that was driving her to be contrary: for two pins she would have included Hunsett in the itinerary, too. Perhaps she was trying to exasperate him into coming to meet her, she wasn't sure: but she was positive that she couldn't care less about it.

'All right, then. Shall I sail?'

'No thank you. If you're sure I'm doing it properly.'

Between them there was a grim atmosphere on that sail up to Southery Staithe, though Stella for her part was resolved not to notice it. Keith had his back to her all the way and answered only monosyllables, paying no atention at all to her exclamations on the scenery. They came to the end of the channel at last, to the narrow dyke leading to the staithe, where an old timber and pantile warehouse offered a reminder of the vanished wherry-trade. Stella made a turn or two in the widest part of the dyke, and was secretly relieved to find that she wouldn't have to tack her way out.

'You see? There's nothing here.'

She smiled at his unrelenting shoulders. 'Where is your poetry, my son? I find this highly evocative.'

'A dyke too narrow to tack in and a slummy old building. That's the fact when you see it straight. That's the reality of Southery.'

'It's the reality of your mood. And your mood is unintelligent.'

'No, it's the fact – the rest is something you add to it.'

'Then why not add something to it instead of parading your lack of imagination. For you, the Taj Mahal could be expressed in tons of stone.'

'Why do you mention the Taj Mahal?'

'Weren't you airing your Buddhist principles?'

'It's true. All this is illusion.'

'But isn't Samsara also Nirvana?'

He didn't try arguing any further, she was being too deliberately crushing: he felt, as she intended him to, the greater subtlety she had to command. But damnation, these kids with their half-baked ideas! They were so proud of their scepticism and yet were the most gullible believers going. Stella shrugged disparagingly. What in the world did they two have in common?

Now the breeze had begun to slacken and their pace became more loitering, slowing at times to a drift when they were hampered by trees. It took them the better part of an hour to get back to the Broad, and when they arrived the wind took off altogether, leaving surfaces like glass. Other yachts lay drifting too, their sails idle or lazily snaking, suggesting taller and more careless lilies against the pastel green reeds. One or another would catch a slant and ripple a few lengths from its position, then its yards would creak helplessly and it would come to a fresh standstill. Stella quoted the verse to herself: painted ships on a painted ocean. It better fitted the world of the Broad than anything its author could have imagined. A motor-cruiser coming up the channel made ripples that spread to either shore, and as they reached each yacht in turn one heard the gentle bump of gaff or boom. The Broad had acoustics that were remarkable: it was a gigantic sounding-board.

'We shall have to break out the Seagull unless things pick up.'

Keith stirred vaguely. He was lying on a seat, his chin resting on the coaming. By Stella's watch it was ten minutes since they last had a waft of breeze, and as yet they were only a couple of hundred yards down the Broad. The sun, too, was burningly hot and came off the surface in a glare.

'If you like I'll use the paddle.'

'That might be an idea.'

He rolled himself off the seat and felt below it for the paddle. Paddling was a slow way of making progress, especially as Keith didn't greatly exert himself, but it was better than sitting still or trying to waggle along with the tiller. Stella smoked, though her lips were dry. She experienced a feeling of great weariness. They seemed to have been too long in the boat, it was growing heavy and tiresome with her. What she wanted now was a wash and the restful gloom of the cottage lounge, a cup of tea from a fresh pot, a laze in the cool and perhaps a book. As for Keith, oh my God! That thirteen years was proving insuperable.

'Shall we . . . do you want to go in?'

Her spirit groaned. 'It's pretty hot out here, isn't it?'

He paddled on for a few strokes, rebuffed, then said: 'There's a mooring over there, beneath those willows . . .'

She looked where he pointed, stifling a sigh. There was indeed a creek, with a promise of shade and a certain privacy.

'All right then. I'll try it once.'

'We won't if you'd rather not . . .'

'For heaven's sake get on with your paddling! This sun is frying me.'

After that he used a little more energy, and they moved with some purpose through the lifeless water. The creek, which was no more than a shallow bay with a toe, was opposite the island and had a bank which looked firm. Stella jiggled them along it until boughs obstructed further progress. She took the rond-anchor ashore herself, she was so impatient for the green shade. The bank was of springy, minty peat, delightfully covered with short, fine grass, and the odour of it rose through her brain so that she immediately began to revive. She drank it in in large, grateful lungfuls, at the same time stretching her cramped limbs. Now it wanted only that cup of tea for one to be thoroughly comfortable again.

'I suppose there's nothing drinkable left in the bag?'

'Oh yes . . . there's a thermos of something.'

'A thermos!' She could hardly credit her ears. But it was true: in their possession they had a large thermos of tea.

15

She drank her tea reverently, one cup after another, there being enough for three apiece in Keith's magnificent utensil. It had the true thermosy flavour even though the milk was packed in separately, but she wasn't in a mood to find any fault with that.

'That's the best tea I've tasted for years and years.'

He gave her a flickering smile, but it was plain that he didn't understand. Tea to Keith was simply a drink and perhaps only a substitute for beer. Well, you couldn't blame him, men were all the same that way. She drew up a cushion and began to relax, feeling that even to smoke would be a mild sacrilege.

'Come and sit down and talk to me.' She placed a cushion on the floorboards near her. Perhaps, after all, she had been rather harsh on the poor kid. Keith sat himself lumpily in his subservient position, not daring to come close enough to rest his shoulder against her knee.

'Now tell me some more about yourself, about your friends and family. Because really I don't know very much about you, do I?'

'There isn't much to know.'

'Yes there is, about everyone. Tell me about your life at Cambridge. Tell me about your swimming.'

He began reluctantly, but Stella was expert at drawing people out, and before long she had him talking freely about himself and his interests. It was as she had supposed; he had led a lonely and somewhat shut-off existence, unhappily at loggerheads with the people who were close to him. He had been brought up by a father who was himself unsociable. Iain Lea-Stephens had been a man exclusively dedicated to his profession. He had married young to the flighty daughter of a Yorkshire 'county' family, and the effect of what had been a *mésalliance* had been to confirm his moroseness. To his son he had been dutiful in a frigid, jealous way. He had provided for him generously in everything except affection. Thus it wasn't very surprising that Keith didn't much mourn his memory, for his father had seemed to him a stranger with whom he had few points of contact. He had also seemed a tyrant; he was determined to have Keith in the firm. It had probably never occurred to him to doubt whether Keith was fitted for such a future.

This was the more unfortunate since Keith himself was full of uncertainty, knowing only what he was not and not what he was. He had vague literary inclinations and he was attracted by philosophy. He could draw rather well but didn't see himself as

72

a painter. He was the sort of young man who above all things needed a liberal education, a careful drawing out and testing of his talents and affinities. Instead he had been guided towards a narrow technical training, and though he had tackled this with integrity he was clearly finding it frustrating. He was haunted by the anxiety of probable failure. It had sapped his confidence, made him shy, had inhibited his personality. Stella understood and was touched afresh. She was sorry now for her selfish surliness.

'And your mother. Has she never been in touch with you?'

Keith had been sitting bolt upright while he was talking. Now, from studying the shimmering Broad, his eyes sank till they fixed on his knees.

'She sent somebody once, a friend. To see what I was like, I suppose. It was at Cambridge, last year. A middle-aged lady. She took me to tea.'

'What did she say to you?'

'Oh, she said she'd heard about me from my mother. My mother had asked her to give me a message . . . that sort of thing.'

'And what was the message?'

'Nothing. Just that she hoped I was getting along. I think the lady got bored with me. She was only with me for about an hour.'

Stella was struck by a suspicion. 'Did she give you her name?'

'No.' Keith's head drooped a little lower.

'Then she might have been your mother?'

'I don't know. She might have been.'

'Poor kid!'

'It didn't matter. After all, it wasn't the same . . .'

But it had been his mother, the rotten bitch, going there in pretence to see how Keith had turned out. So little of a mother that she wouldn't even reveal herself, getting bored in an hour, and letting him see it! What a blow that must have been . . . what a terrible, crushing blow. Stella had idolised her own mother. Her blood seethed as she thought about it.

'But your grandfather – he's quite a decent sort, isn't he?'

'Oh yes. We get on well. He understands a bit about things. He put it to me that I needn't go on with engineering if I didn't want to. But I'm the only one left. And I don't know what else to do.'

'Don't you think it might be wiser to take him up on that?'

Keith squirmed. 'I don't know. It's hard to look at it like that. He was awfully fond of my father, and he built the firm himself. It's such an important thing with him. And Uncle Simon won't go near it.'

'But he's had his life with it and he shouldn't ask more than that. He found his happiness in building it, and in having one son of a mind with him. To want you to carry it on isn't reasonable in the circumstances. You have a right to your own life, and no duty to sacrifice it.'

'I've tried to think it out, Stella . . .'

'I would like to have a talk with your grandfather.'

She hinted at the row that Simon had had with his father, but details of this were apparently unknown to Keith. He had heard only that there had been a 'bust-up' over something that had happened in Norfolk, and that his grandfather and Simon were on very bad terms.

'But they made it up, didn't they?'

Keith's shoulder twitched. 'They did. But there was another row later, when I was at home at Easter. To tell you the truth' – he flushed a little, looking up at her guiltily – 'I thought it better not to tell grandad that I was coming down here.'

'Why not?'

'Well, he thinks Uncle Simon isn't . . . you know! He lives with a woman. It's silly of course. But I love being down here. So I said I was staying with friends so as not to upset grandad.'

'You're a bit deceitful, my pet.'

Keith was quick to defend himself. 'I'm not, not really. It's only because grandad is so peculiar. After all, I don't mind about Uncle Simon. If he were married to Glynda grandad would think it quite proper.'

Stella laughed at his naïvety. Keith must be finding the present subject embarrassing.

74

'Tell me something. Wasn't it Uncle Simon who suggested that you should fib to your grandfather?'

'Yes . . . actually. He did hint at it.'

'I thought I recognized the master's hand.'

They were feeling cooler now in their retired nook beneath sweet-smelling willows. The sun which blazed on the glassy water only freckled them where they lay. Two sails, one vivid crimson, rode their reflections deep in the Broad, and only rarely did a throbbing motor-cruiser pass between them and the reedy island. Stella lowered herself from her seat to the cushions on the floorboards. This was her gesture of contriteness for her earler ill-nature. She drew Keith down beside her, making room for his clumsy largeness; then she took his head between her hands and gently kissed him.

'Now I want you to be good, because we're not entirely private.'

'I'll do anything, Stella . . .'

'For this once you'll be good. I'm not at all sure what I'm to do about you, Keith. So you'll just be good until I've made up my mind.'

He lay quite still, watching her through half-closed eyes, and she hung over him, examining him, her chin on her hand. Close-to his face was handsome, its youthful line even beautiful; the skin was clear and very smooth and the eyes had fine curling lashes. She felt a pang of desire for him but she quickly controlled it. Not yet, and not here, must there be anything of that sort. But she moved over him and lay clasping him, her lips mingling with his, keenly enjoying the sensation of his strong body beneath hers. And they lay so for some minutes in a passionate kiss, her fingers grasping his hair in unconscious cruelty; she could feel his hand moving blindly up and down her back, making an intuitive caress, a clumsy appeal to her ardour. They broke apart, breathing quickly. She thought it had gone rather far. A little more and she wouldn't have been answerable for what she did. She held away for some moments, letting her emotions subside, then she kissed him more briefly, perfunctorily almost.

'You're rather a bear, Keith.'

'Stella, I love you!'

'You don't, but you're a poppet, and a wicked poppet at that.'

'Stella, kiss me . . .'

'My love, you've been kissed quite enough.'

'You're wonderful, Stella!'

'Remember. You're being good.'

She disentangled herself from him and went back to her cushions, and lay cradling his head while she stroked the dishevelled hair. His lips kissed her repeatedly; she made way for them a little. Her breast looked very white against the tanned cheek pressed to it.

'What possessed you to read my books, young man?'

She twisted his head to make him look up at her.

'Your picture . . . I saw it. In one of the magazines.'

'My picture! Which one?'

'It appeared in *Bookman*. I saw it . . . I thought then . . .'

'You didn't fall in love with a picture?'

'I knew. And then I met you. It just had to be.'

Not for the first time in her dealings with Keith Stella was taken aback: she had never supposed that the picture in *Bookman* would sweep young men off their feet. It showed her in discrete evening wear at a publisher's reception, one of several she had attended to publicise the Justin book. Still, it wasn't unflattering to have made an impression by a photograph. She wondered if there were other youths secretly cherishing a passion for her.

'And then you started to read my books?'

'Yes . . . I got one from a library.'

'Which one?'

'*The Deathless Country.*'

That was a harmless enough beginning. It related the soul-searchings of a country girl who, after a torrid session in town, had returned to Dorset to rediscover her peace of mind.

'And then?'

'I don't know. But I read them, one by one. I was going to

write you once. Then I thought it would seem silly.'

'So in effect I'm an old flame of yours?'

'I told you, it's true. I love you terribly.'

'You're in love with love, but I can't say that I blame you.'

'I'm in love with you. You're beautiful, unbearable . . .'

She remained a while basking in this pitch of adoration, resting her cheek on the head that lay nestled in her bosom. There was no doubt that this was an extraordinarily romantic affair; his having first fallen for her picture gave it quite a classic touch. And here, on the Broad, it had the perfect setting for its development. On their shallop in enchanted waters they pursued their soft dalliance. Spenser, had he been a modern, would have seen it and approved, and would have taken in his stride the murmur and wash of passing pleasure boats. She patted Keith on the shoulder. The lad had imagination, after all.

16

After supper Simon rang:

'It's regatta day tomorrow.'

Stella made a face. 'Do I fly a flag or something?'

She heard him chuckle. 'You can if you like. There's a flagstaff at the summerhouse. But I'm mooring *Sunbird* on the Broad and I was wondering if you would care to join us.'

'What to do?'

'Don't sound so suspicious! You can go racing if that would amuse. According to Keith you're pretty handy, and there will be two races for *Lutestring*. Or you can do like the rest of us and laze around and watch. There's plenty of room on *Sunbird*, and I can answer for the commissariat.'

'Thank Keith for his compliment.' (The fool, why couldn't he keep his mouth shut?)

'Oh, he was loud in your praises. You have quite dazzled Master Keith.'

'I made him sit and watch me sail, if that's what you mean. At first I don't think he had any great opinion of me.'

'Well, that's as may be, but he's a big fan now. But you'll come along, my dear, won't you? I look on you as one of the party.'

'All right, I'll come.'

'That's the spirit. *Sunbird* is leaving at ten sharp.'

'I'll join you later, in the dinghy.'

'You'll find us moored next to the committee-boat.'

She hung up and returned to some chores she was engaged with. Damn Simon! Why did he have to be so insistent about Keith? He had deliberately sought for a way to drag him into the conversation, seizing on whatever could be interpreted as suggestive in their relations. It was unnecessary, it was in bad taste to keep harping on the subject – and inconsistent too; not what one would expect of Simon. Could it be that she was still ignorant of the interplay going on at Lazy Waters? Had some new twist been given to the plot that required her continued interest in Keith?

Glynda, she thought; it must be Glynda again; her jealousy had spilled over from Dawn to Stella. Glynda must have heard or guessed something of the flirtatious passage on Simon's motor cruiser, and now it devolved on Simon to see that Stella was firmly tagged. Yes; that had to be it; and she felt a momentary sympathy for Simon. But then the sympathy turned to scorn as she considered his weakness. He was letting Glynda push him around when in fact he had only to put his foot down: an ultimatum sternly delivered, and she must either climb down or get to hell. He wasn't in love with her, he'd said so, she was there purely on her merits; so why was he descending to these Machiavellian tactics – did he enjoy them for their own sake?

When the chores were finished and her clutter cleared away Stella stuffed some cigarettes in her cardigan pocket and went down to the summerhouse. There, still laid out on the table, were the synopsis and sheets of her abortive novel, and she looked them over coolly from what seemed an enormous distance. Thank the Lord she hadn't gone any further with that one! It was easy to see how that it would have been a resounding flop. One couldn't write like that, in the grip of personal emotions, it could only be done objectively when the emotions were tidied up. The summerhouse had a grate; Stella crumpled the papers into it. When they had burned she broke up the ashes and riddled them into the pan below. Then she carried them to the veranda and tipped them over into the water – and so much for Justin! She felt she had cauterised a wound.

The dinghy was still moored at the staithe and the calm evening was inviting; the sun had descended behind trees to leave a cool, pellucid light. An evening breeze had sprung up, tracing cat's-paws on the surface, and a few small sails had come out to take advantage of it. Stella decided it would suit her mood to be out there too. She went down to the dinghy and raised its friendly brown sail. The breeze was light, but she didn't mind, it seemed the hour to be slowly drifting; she stretched herself on the floorboards and let the boat sail as it would. It was a novel experience. The dinghy enclosed her like a cradle. Its sail mounted the sky above her as huge as the sail of a wherry. Their progress was silent, a slow, rippleless gliding, and gave an impression of vast detachment from all the world beside.

In this way she went drifting round the island in the Broad, until the need to begin tacking brought an end to her dreamlike passage. Also the breeze, which had been adequate to send her over the Broad, now had to be nursed with care if it was to be deceived into bringing her back again. She got up on the seat and began to sail with more attention. Another dinghy, with a blue sail, was slowly crossing the Broad ahead of her. Then she noticed, bearing towards her with easy strokes of his oars, her would-be gardener, Sam Fulcher, in his double-ended rowboat. She put about. She went off in a tack away from the Alderford corner. She had no intention of inviting another encounter with this detestable fellow. After her turn she saw him pause, then alter course to keep towards her, and she was glad when a slant of breeze came to speed her away from his pursuit.

But he continued to hang about where she would have to pass by him. Her anger rose as she saw this: Simon had promised to deal with the brute! She made a turn or two in the channel, hoping to wear out his patience, but still he remained, his oars levelled, now and then dipping them to hold his place. Very well: she thought she knew a trick worth two of that. There was a passage through the reed islands outflanking the one that Fulcher was guarding. She had noticed it the day before and thought it might be worth exploring, and though she was ignorant of where it came out, yet it had to be in the Alderford direction. She retracted her plate a little and tacked towards the reeds. She found the passage quite easily and was able to lay it on a close haul. She knew that Fulcher must have seen her but she doubted his nerve to come in pursuit, and she wasn't too upset when the breeze tailed away and she was obliged to take to her oars.

But her escape route led her into a different sort of encounter, for on turning a bend she found her way blocked by the houseboat of the angler. There was room for her to push by, but he had to raise his line for her, so she could scarcely escape without some exchange of pleasantries. He gave her a friendly grimace.

'You're the first person to come *that* way.'

'I'm awfully sorry. I didn't mean to disturb you.'

'Oh, it doesn't matter, the fish have gone off the feed anyway. They usually do about now, and then come on again at midnight. Would you like to see my catch?'

Without waiting for her reply he hoisted on the cord of his keep-net, and dragged to the surface a bag of fish which, even to Stella's blank ignorance, looked a haul of some magnificence. He inspected it complacently.

'They're rudd, those beauties with red fins. And roach, and bream. And that perch is going on two pounds. I pulled out a tench on Saturday, and a rare fight he gave me. This is a prime spot for fish. They run through the channel into the Broad.'

'How many would there be?' Stella gazed with fascination at

the struggling netful. Some of the fish looked veritable monsters and their fins were a beautiful glowing ruby.

'I haven't weighed in yet. Getting on for four stone, it wouldn't surprise me.'

'But how many fish?'

He heaved bulky shoulders. 'Maybe fifty, more or less.'

He let them sink slowly out of sight, then winked at her and took out a pipe. He was a big, solidly-built man, probably nearer fifty than forty. He had a likeable, rugged face with a determined, square jaw, a strong nose, emphatic brows and hair lightly touched with grey. He wore an ancient tweed jacket and a yet older, more shapeless hat, and was studying her amusedly with twinkling, greenish eyes. For some reason Stella said to herself: country GP.

'And how do you like the Broads, Miss Rushton?'

She was startled. 'You know my name?'

'Mmn.' He nodded over lighting his pipe. 'I haven't read your books, I'm afraid to say. But I have seen them reviewed.'

'Then you must think them profitless, vapid and stupid.'

'I might. But I've read a lot of reviews.'

'You're in publishing, are you?'

'Good Lord, no! But I do a bit of reading. When they let me have the time.'

Now she was convinced that her guess had been correct, because 'when they let me have the time' was a favourite expression of her father's. He too liked reading when the evening surgery closed its doors – with one eye on the clock and an ear on the telephone. He used to devour crime fiction at the rate of one title per sitting.

'You read detective novels, do you?'

'Mmn.' His eyes twinkled roguishly. 'And straight novels too . . . thought they're apt to be profitless, vapid and stupid.'

'What have you got on board?' she challenged him.

'Oh, an odd sort of collection. You can come and see if you like. You are welcome to borrow what's there.'

She hesitated but only for the moment before hitching her

dinghy to the houseboat. There was nothing in the least predatory about this amused, pacific man. He had that degree of modest charm – his bedside manner, no doubt – that in an indefinable way impressed one as being deeply understanding. His patients were lucky people, she thought; he was the very best type of country GP.

The houseboat was rectangular in shape and much too large for one person. One boarded it by a landing well and went through a sliding door into a lounge. This was a spacious cabin furnished with a low table and comfortable chairs, having a fitted sideboard, a bookcase and a bureau, the latter with a barometer and a clock mounted over it. The floor was carpeted, and a gas fire offered comfort for chill evenings; altogether, it seemed more of a turn-out than one might expect an angler to inhabit. He grinned at her silent appraisal and, though it was unnecessary, switched on a light.

'I don't own this of course – I'm not in the supertax bracket.'

'It looks a lovely boat.'

'It belongs to a good friend of mine.'

'It's nice to have friends with possessions, too.'

He chuckled, dropping into a chair. 'Those are my books, on the top shelf.'

She examined them with curiosity. They were not at all what she had anticipated. There were indeed a handful of paperback Simenons but these formed only a small part of the parcel. The rest comprised a selection of Broads books by such as Davies, Suffling and Patterson, a number of classics in translation and two volumes of *Notable British Trials*. It was such a disparate collection that Stella could make nothing of it. She thought that her angler was a man with either a broad or a very discursive intellect. After a little tasting around she selected Patterson's *Through Broadland in a Breydon Punt*.

'Since you are so kind, I would like to borrow this.'

'Don't mention it, Miss Rushton. I shall be here for another week.'

'I'll take care to return it before then.' She paused. 'Shouldn't we be introduced?'

He blew a casual but perfect smoke ring. 'George,' he said carefully.

She waited, but that apparently was all she was going to get. All right, she thought, all right, my boy. Then she was aware of the mild eyes fixed quizzically upon her, and she felt herself flushing: he knew exactly what she was thinking.

'George what?' she asked furiously.

'Just "George" in these parts. When I'm on holiday I leave the rest of me behind.'

'I don't think that's fair. You knew who I was.'

He nodded. 'But I'm a nobody. So be a sport and let me stay anonymous.'

'You're a GP, aren't you?'

He smiled slowly, hesitatingly. 'You're an observant woman, Miss Rushton. What made you guess that?'

'Because my father is one too, so I happen to know the type.'

'Good.' He puffed at his pipe. 'I'll have to get hold of some of your books.'

Stella was still nettled but she felt she had settled that point: her instinct had been true, she could almost smell the ether. She leaned against the bureau enjoying her little moment of triumph. Against her will, she was being forced to admit that George had a very disturbing effect on her.

'Whereabout do you practise?'

His smile became almost angelic. 'No, Miss Rushton, you've gone far enough. Let me stay my holiday self.'

'I could find out, you know.'

'Yes, of course. But you won't, will you? We fellows deserve our holidays. We're sometimes darned lucky to get them.'

'I still think you're being mean.'

'No you don't, not really.'

'Well, I would if it were someone else.'

He laughed. 'For that, I'm going to offer you a drink.'

When at last she rowed away the disturbed feeling was far from quieted, and not looking where she was going she twice had brushes with the reeds. It was odd. George had been there all the time she was at the cottage. How could Stella, for so long, have missed this intriguing element in her little world?

17

On arriving back at the summerhouse she drew the mosquito netting across the veranda, then lit the brass ship's lamp that hung on the wall. The evening breeze had died too, leaving the twilight perfectly still, and a ghostly carpet of smoke mist lay in bands over the water. She sat broodingly watching it and drinking in the night sounds. The light of the lamp attracted moths to the net from all directions. Some were enormous, some small and delicate, but all had fiery, gem-like eyes, and as they buzzed and fluttered they stared in at her with fierce, choleric intentness. Other sounds she identified slowly: the sudden plunge of a fish, the rustle of a coypu or a water rat, an angry snicker which she attributed to an otter.

Then she heard another sound, a low, continuous splashing. It sounded as though it were coming towards her down the mist-covered waterway. Once or twice its beat hesitated, as though what made it had stopped to listen, but then it continued to advance with a steady, intent rhythm. She strained her eyes to pierce the mist for a glimpse of the origin of the sound. She felt a tingle of apprehension at its unafraid approach. Surely there was nothing on the Broad that could be regarded as dangerous – some nocturnal horror akin to the monsters of the Scottish lochs? At last she made out a dark object moving slowly in the water; and rowing it along what at first appeared to be two thick, pale tentacles. With a gust of relief she identified this startling phenomenon as a swimmer, and then immediately she understood: of course, it was Keith. She pushed the net aside. She went out on the veranda. She saw him drag himself out on the staithe near the gently rocking dinghy.

'What on *earth* are you up to?'

He remained for a moment kneeling, shaking off the weakness induced by immersion. Then he pulled himself to his feet. He stood dripping and slapping his ears.

'I was out swimming . . . I saw your light. I thought I'd come in this direction.'

He was on the shiver, and had a look more than usually pathetic. He was wearing a pair of red trunks that sagged unfortunately at the stomach, and his hair was plastered in a spiky fringe from which water dribbled into his eyes.

'Well – you'd better come up. I keep a towel here, fortunately.'

'It doesn't matter. I'm going to swim back to the house in any case.'

'Your teeth are chattering, you nitwit. You'll come and dry yourself this minute. And if you do any more swimming tonight, you're a fool.'

'I'm used to it, Stella . . .'

'Keith, sometimes I despair of you.'

He came wetly up the steps and stood dripping in the doorway. She thrust him the hand-towel which, with a bit of soap, she'd brought to the summerhouse. He began to use it with simulated vigour, still standing in the doorway, and she looked round to find him something to throw over his shoulders. In effect there was only a raincoat which she had installed there for insurance; it was large for her, but didn't look much to cover Keith's generous six foot.

'I don't know what we're going to do with you. You'll have to be swathed in blankets. I've no clothes at the cottage that will be of any use.'

'I'm going to swim back, I tell you. You don't understand. Naturally you shiver when you get out, but that doesn't mean a thing.'

'Yes it does. It means you're chilled.'

'But you're all right if you stop in. Honestly, Stella, I haven't been far. I just came . . . through the Broad.'

'Meaning you came to see me?'

'I don't know . . . I wanted . . .'

She looked him over, nodding her head. He kept scrubbing away with the towel. So he had come to see her, come blindly seeking the thing he wanted. And she was there. And they were alone. And the dark night lay about them. Like Leander, he had swum his Hellespont to gain his Hero. She wondered if the original Hero had met her swain with a towel, and whether his teeth had been chattering as he stood dripping water everywhere.

'Dry yourself for heaven's sake. That's the least you can do.'

'Yes, Stella. I'm sorry . . .'

'And you'd better shut the door.'

He pulled it shut, fumbling the latch. She went across to the lamp. For a moment she stood eyeing him. Then she turned down the light.

18

She was surprised to find how quickly Keith went out of her head – like an eaten meal, for instance, or the clearing-up after it. When she had returned to the cottage and put herself to bed only a complacent languidness reminded her that he had existed. She felt unrepentant about this. She had no duty to be thinking about him. Whatever she was to him, he was to her only a delectable bedfellow. And now that her desire had been satisfied, her curiosity sated, it would be hypocritical to try to lend the matter a significance it didn't possess. Rather, if it came to measuring significance, it was the angler, George, who claimed her attention. He had scarcely been out of her thoughts and she had gone to sleep thinking about him. He was by every standard disturbing; she wondered if he were married. He must be a widower, she decided, taking one thing with another. If he were married his wife would hardly release him for holidays of this sort, though a man like George must surely have been married at some time. She found the conclusion a pleasing one and she was sent to sleep by its flattery.

The smoke mist of the evening had promised another fine day and other than a skein of high stratus the morrow verified its portent. Stella wasted no time in going down to the dinghy, and from the staithe could see sails already moving on the Broad. She made sail and reached away down her bay of waterlilies. She took care to go close to the white-painted houseboat. George was sitting in the well in his familiar position, wearing the same old jacket and disreputable hat. He lifted the latter and smiled across to her. She fetched up into the wind. She asked, incredulously:

'Have you been fishing all night, then?'

His smile became a chuckle. 'No, I'm not that crazy. I'd had a good day, you remember, so I decided to turn in.'

'Did you weigh them?'

'Of course. There were fifty-four pounds. That bream was the best one, but I had a rudd going two.'

'Is that big for a rudd?'

'Well . . . yes! It's getting large. You hear stories of three-pounders, but you never meet a man who's caught one.'

He winked at her, and by this light she saw that his eyes were in fact hazel, and that they had an engaging way of screwing up when the sun fell on them. She scooped some wind in her sail to prevent the dinghy from edging away, and he watched the manoeuvre with an approving sort of interest.

'Are you going to watch the regatta?' – she nodded towards his rowing dinghy.

'Mmn. I may do.' His broad shoulders twitched. 'You will be on *Sunbird*, will you, with Mr Lea-Stephens?'

'Yes – do you know him?'

'Oh . . . I've seen him about here.'

A suspicion dawned on Stella at the evasive form of this answer and she looked at him quickly, her eyes challenging his. Could it be – was it possible – that 'George' was Keith's grandfather, posted here in disguise to keep an eye on Lazy Waters? But she realised at once that such a notion was fantastic. George could be no more than fifty and Simon wasn't much younger. She thought: my girl, you have a guilty conscience, and let the look tail off with the best grace she could.

'I thought we had decided that I was a GP.'

Once more the damnable fellow had read her thoughts like a book! She pouted.

'I'm not sure. You're very mysterious for a GP.'

'That probably comes of being so frank all the rest of the year.'

He was laughing at her now, and she could feel her colour rising. Oh hell! She was behaving to him as Keith behaved to her. She snapped:

'Well, you know a lot more people here than know you!'

His grin broadened. 'That comes of being anonymous, doesn't it?'

'I think there's something phoney about you.'

'You don't think anything of the sort.'

'How do *you* know what I think?'

'A person's eyes tell you that.'

'George, I'm going to hate you before we're finished.'

He tipped his hat over his eye. 'You wouldn't like some coffee?' he asked.

And there it was again – she couldn't be seriously angry with George. He was altogether too big, too amused, too understanding. She accepted his cup of coffee, scalding hot from the galley, and sat drinking it in the dinghy while he arranged his tackle for a fresh cast.

'Do you always have fishing holidays?' she asked him.

'Not always.' He reeled in his slack; his float, a long porcupine quill, showed only a notch of luminous yellow. 'But it's the most relaxing pastime I know of . . . and it keeps the mind supple. You may think that anglers just sit, but they always sit and think. There's no substitute for it when it comes to filling a keep-net.'

'I shouldn't have thought much skill was needed to outwit a fish.'

'I'll lend you a rod. That will teach you more respect for them. Fish have everything in their favour with the exception of brains – those are the angler's weapon. He uses brains against the odds.'

'And what does your wife think of your going off like this?'

'Perhaps my wife had business to attend to.' His lips curled just a little.

'I'm being nosey, aren't I?'

'Of course you are, Miss Rushton.'

'Call me Stella, you brute.'

'Yes, Miss Rushton. Stella.'

She finished her coffee and sailed off with a twinge of regret, but was absurdly pleased on looking back to catch him watching her progress. She felt a most decided itch to know more about George; she knew she wouldn't be satisfied until she had probed that upsetting personality.

She had no trouble in identifying *Sunbird*, which Simon kept moored in a cut at Alderford. She was anchored with others in a line of craft on either side of the committee houseboat. She was a wherry-yacht, a type that had been popular at the turn of the century, a species of long, broad-beamed vessel with a straight stem and ranging counter. They were rigged in wherry-fashion with a tremendous unstayed mast, having at its head, above painting and gilding, a traditional vane in the shape of a Welsh girl. A single loose-footed gaff sail gave these monsters a close-winded performance, and because their masts were counterbalanced they could shoot bridges on the run. *Sunbird* was a notable example of the class. Dressed overall in bunting she made an eye-catching spectacle. With her velvety-white topsides, gilded cove and long run of mahogany coaming, she looked splendidly regal: a very proper boat for a regatta.

Before joining her, Stella made a run down the line of battle. A number of other fine craft had assembled on the Broad. A wherry, shorn of its mast, had been fitted for the accomodation of spectators, and clusters of yachts and motor cruisers had dropped their mud-weights beyond the channel. They were dressed, and they dressed the Broad. It resembled a great marine flower-garden. And framing the bunting and the sails were the green reeds and an infinite sky.

She scudded back to *Sunbird*, where she had already been sighted, and moored the dinghy along with the small craft that accompanied the great yacht. Keith sprang to hand her aboard, his smoky eyes hanging on hers; but she thanked him very coolly and set him to tidy the dinghy's sail. Simon and his guests were lounging in deckchairs on the counter-deck, over which had been erected a gay striped awning. Glasses, bottles and a container of ice stood handily on a table, and Simon motioned to them enquiringly as he rose to welcome her.

'Thank you Simon, a shandy.'

He mixed one for her and added the ice. He was smiling to himself as though he felt particularly pleased. Stella glanced round the deck and noted the disposition of the company. She saw that Dawn and Jeff Simpson were seated together, and a little apart.

'We need a shade more breeze, my dear. And then everything will be perfect.'

'You look radiant, Simon.'

He laughed as he handed her glass. 'I keep checking on my blessings and just now I seem to have plenty. I doubt if I have a care in the world at the moment.'

He sat her down in a chair between himself and Jill Shore, with Glynda on his other side, looking placid in hideous sunglasses. Woody, he told her, had taken off for a spin in the launch, to loll around in which was becoming a favourite pastime. In half an hour the racing was due to begin. He pointed out the triangular course, which would take the yachts round the island. Perhaps the only discordant note on the after-deck was sounded by another unlucky clash of raiment, both Dawn and Glynda having chosen to grace the occasion in towelling sunsuits. Stella felt it was not by chance that they sat with their backs to each other.

Keith came back quietly to squat on a cushion on the deck. He was doing his best, Stella could see, to keep his eyes from being drawn to her. He picked up a pair of binoculars that stood by Simon's chair and zealously examined the craft moored on the opposite side of the channel.

'Are you two thinking of doing some racing?' Simon's smile was insidious and much too knowing. Stella took a long pull from her glass before replying:

'No, I don't think so. What about you and Glynda?'

Glynda stirred herself to say coldly: 'I think that sailing is a silly idea.'

'Perhaps Jill would crew you, Simon.'

Jill looked rather alarmed. 'I don't know enough about it.' She took a sudden interest in a passing cruiser.

'Then what about Dawn?'

'My dear, quite frankly I'm not a racing type.' Simon laughed carefully and was firmly unembarrassed. 'I prefer sailing for its own sake and not as a form of competition. I do my racing spontaneously. It's only a small part of the fun.'

Keith said: 'I'll put us down for the White Boats if you like.'

'No, my pet. I'm like Simon. I do my racing spontaneously.'

'I've swotted up the rules. I'm pretty certain we'd do well.'

'And I'm pretty certain we wouldn't, so we won't put the matter to test.'

The racing began and then there was an object for their attention, though in all honesty Stella could find little in it to stir the blood. As a spectacle it had charm but as a drama not very much, and she quickly became bored with watching for relative changes of position. This was especially so in the handicap races, for there not even the helmsmen had a clear notion of their placings; while in the class races, in which the boats were alike as peas, it seemed a matter of huge indifference that one or other should come in first. But the spectacle remained: the Broad was kept alive with graceful movement. Stella began to enjoy it more when she began to notice it less, when in fact it became a background to a pleasant picnic on the Broad.

Before long, Woody joined them. He handled the launch without much finesse, and Stella caught Simon frowning at a rub on the beautiful varnish. It seemed as much as Woody could do to haul his large body aboard the yacht, and when he'd managed it he dropped into a deckchair and pleaded feebly for a drink. Simon poured one; Woody downed it in a couple of quick gulps. Then he lay back in the chair and stared dreamily at the distance.

'It gets me down!' he said to Stella. 'I'll never last the pace, girlo. I've been watching them sail those dinghies till I nearly collapsed with fatigue.'

'You'll have to wear blinkers, Woody.'

'I close my eyes when it gets too bad. But I can't close my eyes to everything, that's the worst of it, girlo.'

Stella looked at him questioningly. She thought that Woody had used a certain emphasis. But now he had closed his eyes and was looking a picture of exhaustion.

Lunch was served in the saloon, a lobster salad with fresh strawberries to follow. After the glare of the light on the Broad the saloon appeared refreshingly dim. Stella admired the mahogany of the coamings and the two inbuilt sideboards; she imagined it was this wood that helped to give yachts their slightly sweet, distinctive odour. By no design of her own she was sitting between Keith and Simon, and she was annoyed to find that Simon expected her to give her attention to his nephew. Keith however was keeping quiet, even if he tended to look the more for it: Stella snubbed him without mercy and talked to Woody throughout the meal.

After the coffee she found herself restless and on pins to be off. She was weary of remaining a spectator of all the sailing going on around her, weary also of Simon's subtle – and sometimes unsubtle – innuendos. He seemed more than ever resolved on drawing attention to Keith's infatuation. Stella was certain that by now even Ruby, the maid, must be aware of it. Dawn was cutting her like fury, Glynda watching her with calculation, Jill was being the perfect secretary and only Jeff (bless him!) oblivious to the situation. What Woody thought about it was the usual close secret. His big, amiable, creased face was a mask that gave nothing away.

'I think I'll go for a spin in the dinghy,' she said to no one in particular; but Simon, damn his eyes, was only waiting for a chance to pounce.

'Why not take *Lutestring* so that I can get some photographs of her?'

'No thanks. I don't think I could manage her on my own.'

'But my dear, Keith will oblige. And you'll be doing me a real favour. I've been wanting to take some pictures of her to make a pair for my flat.'

If in the end she assented, then it was out of pure defiance. Very well – she'd let them see she wasn't scared to snatch Keith from under their noses! She wondered if Simon would be so damned pleased if he knew how indifferent she really was, or how unlikely it was that this stupid affair would last the week out. She sent Keith to prepare the halfdecker, she took a sudden interest in Simon's camera. She made him show it to her and explain it while she hung intimately on his shoulder. From Glynda in the background she could feel currents of sheer hatred, and she continued to bask in these until Keith had set sail. Perhaps that would take a little of the self-satisfaction out of Simon.

A race was just starting so she waited for the yachts to get away, then she put in a few turns for the benefit of the camera. She gave him *Lutestring* sailing free, on the reach and close-hauled, then, on instructions, came in close while he took shots of boat and crew.

'Right you are – that's the lot. Now you can go and amuse yourselves!'

She saw Keith flushing up and caught a sneering look on Glynda's face. She put her helm up directly, to send the halfdecker driving across the channel. And to hell with the whole boiling of them! Why should she care tuppence what they thought? Put them together, and they would scarcely muster the solid qualities of a man like George.

19

She found a gap in the flotilla opposite through which she could just slide *Lutestring*; then they were away from the prying eyes and binoculars of the wherry-yacht. Keith was facing forward and trying to squeeze himself up small – knowing well enough, the poor innocent, that at the moment he was just an irritant. She took a long sweep behind the screen which the moored craft offered. Slowly her annoyance faded in the pleasure of handling the beautiful halfdecker. She sailed a line down the Broad which might have been traced with a rule, and succeeded in laying the island before the racing fleet snapped at her heels.

'Would you like to take her now?' She felt a twinge of remorse towards Keith. He looked so thoroughly crushed and helpless; she was afraid he might be in tears.

'I'll take her if you want me to.'

'I do. I would like a turn with the jib.'

She turned into the wind and handed him the helm.

'Where did you think of going?'

'It's up to you. You're the skipper now, my lad.'

'I think we'd better go Alderford way. Then we shan't get mixed up with the racing.'

She made the further concession of sitting well down towards him, since a perch up forward was not essential to crewing; but at first he pretended to give all his attention to the sailing, his eye now on the throat, now on the burgee. She let him go his own way, she settled down to enjoy the sail. The channel to Alderford was fresh to her and appeared to be well worth exploring. An arm of the Broad, it ended in a tree-lined dyke leading to the village, but several interesting creeks turned off it, giving glimpses of staithes and old thatched boathouses.

'We won't go into the dyke, will we?'

Stella shook her head. 'Rather not. It would probably mean the paddle, and there's no pleasure in that.'

'We could go back and down the river.'

'Do you think we would stick in one of the creeks?'

'Well . . . I know one with plenty of water. But I thought you wanted to sail.'

She did, but she wanted to be nice to Keith, too. When she thought about him the twinge of remorse continued to nag her. He was a pawn, the poor devil, just a pawn of his uncle Simon's, and Stella herself was doing precious little to allay the sting of it. In a way she was treating him just as badly as his mother had done: she was letting him see, far too clearly, that he meant nothing to her. And Keith, she was afraid, was fatally sensitive. She couldn't suppose it didn't hurt him.

The creek he had chosen was one of those leading to a boathouse, but this and the staithe beside it looked comfortably neglected. In a corner lay a sunken yacht with only its deck and coamings showing, an ancient, fixed-top relic, left to moulder in the mud; in the boathouse one could see another, seemingly of like vintage, while in a cut overgrown with vegetation rested the carcase of a wherry. Fifty, sixty years ago this had probably been a busy staithe, but the passing of the wherries had fated it to a slow decay.

'I wonder if that yacht is ever used.'

Stella was much taken with the place. And the yacht in the boathouse, though shabby and archaic, had a personality that she found intriguing.

'We can look at it if you like. I don't suppose anyone will mind.'

'Do you think so?'

'Why not?'

'It's on your head, my son.'

She could sense his pleasure with the idea of the venture so she let him take the initiative. The boathouse was a dark and repulsively grimy place with moss quilting the slipping thatch of its roof. Inside the splined footways were crazy and in part rotted away; Keith went ahead of her, proud of his agility, then returned to lend her a hand.

'She's the sort of old-timer that you see in early photographs.'

'I know. I was looking at some last night.'

'She must be a hundred . . . just look at her bowsprit! And her decks are planked-up. And what a stick she's got on her . . .'

She was about thirty-five feet long and had a beam that seemed prodigious, schooner-bowed, long in the counter and with at least six inches of toe-rail. Her cabin roof looked very squat, as though it were crouching towards the decks, and her windows were flat ellipses that had no business with opening and closing. The twin doors from the well were not locked; Stella unlatched them and hooked them open. The hatch above them was so stiff that she was obliged to leave it closed. Below, down two steps, was a low but very roomy cabin, a long one, on the berths of which people had doubtless slept end-to-end. It was lined with dirty embossed paper and smelt dry if stuffy. It was fitted with numerous drawers and lockers and – surprise! – a tiny piano. She passed through it into a short passage, on one side of which was a toilet; she was obliged to smile at the mighty throne and at the fluting and flowers of the washbasin; then into a smaller cabin fitted with three berths and a dressing-table, which she was able to identify at once as 'the cabin for the ladies'.

'Come and look in the forepeak.'

She climbed back on deck through the companion-hatch. In the forepeak Keith was admiring its two pipe-cots and an enormous, rusty cooker.

'This would be the crew's quarters, the skipper and the cook. It was like this on *Sunbird* before Uncle Simon modernised it.'

'It must be hell down there when you're cooking dinner.'

'I don't know. It's rather fun.'

Keith climbed out looking scruffy and brushing his trousers with his hands.

'She's sound, you can smell that. What a shame to leave her here to rot.'

'It would cost you a fortune to put her in commission.'

'I'm not so sure. And I'm coming into some cash when I'm twenty-one.'

'You'll want something handier, more modern.'

'Yes, I suppose that's possible. But it would be something to tackle this one – to restore her, not modernise her.'

He ran his hand caressingly over the blistered varnish of the coaming, and she was touched by the affection he seemed to feel for the old boat. She said, with sudden inspiration:

'You'd want to do it yourself, wouldn't you?'

He leaned his head on one side. 'Yes . . . I would like to have a go.'

Boats, she said to herself: and that could be the answer, young man. They could represent that alternative vocation towards which he was blindly feeling. Neither mechanical things on the one hand nor abstract on the other, but an absorbing physical expression of that between thinking and dreaming: boats. And why shouldn't Keith become a designer and builder of boats?

'What is it exactly that your grandfather's firm manufactures?'

'Oh, repetition products, tube, and light power units.'

'Would it take much to persuade him to start a marine division?'

He looked at her quickly. 'Marine power units, perhaps.'

'Well, that would be a start.' She could see that the idea interested him. He continued staring at her, half-questioning, half-doubtful. 'After engines you might persuade him to go in for hulls – light alloys, glass-fibre: make it sound like engineering.'

'But I'm not much interested in light alloys and glass-fibre.'

'Never mind that, you idiot. The rest can come later. After all, one day you're going to run that firm yourself, and then you can turn it over to boats as fast as you like.'

'There seems an awful big gap between *this* and extrusions.'

'Isn't the gap even bigger between extrusions and yourself?'

She had hit on it, she knew. He became silent and distant, forgetting even herself in his contemplation of the proposition.

When at last after much frowning he appeared to notice her presence again, it was only to ask her suddenly:

'Is that what you would do?'

She laughed and left him to mull it over by himself – it was close in the boathouse, she was glad to get outside again. She was pleased with herself, she felt she had been rather clever. She had known Keith for only two days and already she had solved his insoluble problem. She returned to the halfdecker and stretched herself out in the sun. The fresh air, along with Simon's champagne, was making her feel foolish and sleepy. From the distance she heard the gun which signalled the start or end of a race, then the murmur of a passing motor-cruiser, then nothing but the twitter of sedge-warblers. It was the sound of a different engine which made her open her eyes with a start. She recognised it directly. It was the throb of the launch's diesel. She caught sight of the launch creeping along the channel towards Alderford. Simon was driving it alone. His eyes were turned towards the halfdecker. He was hardly out of sight before she saw him coming back again, but this time he had opened the throttle and was charging by in a swathe of wash. And glaring after him furiously, she became aware of someone else. Fulcher was paddling across the creek-mouth. And he too was interested in the halfdecker.

20

When they returned to *Sunbird* she didn't openly accuse Simon of spying, but she treated him with a coolness that he could scarcely fail to understand. Tea was being served and she went pointedly to sit by Woody; then later she attached herself to Jill Shore, who seemed rather nervous to receive Stella's patronage. Happily Keith had learned his lesson and felt less compelled to hang around her. After tea he took a rod to the foredeck, and appeared quite content to fish. The regatta continued with rowing and novelty races, followed by a procession of decorated boats, and ended with a handsome display of fireworks from a float towed into the channel. Then after a drink, Stella left, leaving the others to spend the night on board. She rowed home over a darkened Broad which strangely echoed the strokes of her oars.

It happened only by chance that she noticed an envelope pushed through her door; entering the cottage she had missed it, but saw it on returning to check the bolt. She examined the envelope with puzzlement for it bore no stamp or postmark; merely her Christian name, and this scrawled in block capitals. She tore it open. The sheet inside was also scrawled with capitals. For a moment or so she failed to grasp the import of them. She read:

'STELLA A FRIENDLY WARNING YOU'LL BE WISE IF YOU DROP KEITH NO NAMES NO PACK DRILL KEEP THIS LETTER TO YOURSELF I'M SERIOUS ABOUT THIS DON'T DO SOMETHING YOU'LL REGRET A WELLWISHER'

When their meaning did sink in she could feel herself turning red and white with anger. She crushed the letter into a ball and hurled it across the room. Who – who could have sent her such a filthy and insulting thing? Who thought they had the right to offer her an affront like that? It was like a blow in the dark, a cowardly, secret attack. It made her clench her fists until the nails almost drew blood. She marched up and down the room in a passion of rage, feeling in some way defiled by this poisonous invasion of her privacy.

'Keep calm, Stella Rushton, keep calm and think.'

She chanted the words aloud to herself, but it was some time before she could obey them. She felt like screaming every time she remembered the words addressed to her: so insulting, so threatening, so hypocritical they were! What unspeakable person could have done this to her? Was it one of Simon's tricks – Dawn's wretched revenge? Had Glynda got it in for her – Woody – Jill Shore? They all seemed bad and wicked enough for this. They were intriguers every one, degenerate, spiteful,

99

worthless people. But – and she realised this in a panic – it didn't stop with them. It could be some malign person outside the orbit of Lazy Waters. It could be Fulcher, for instance, who was always prying around, or . . . she felt like being sick. It might be George. It could easily be him.

She threw herself on the settee and clutched her head between her hands. She must calm herself somehow and get this matter sorted out. Until she did everyone around her would be a target for her suspicion, she wouldn't dare trust anyone: somehow she had to narrow it down. There was the element of opportunity, that had to be considered. The letter hadn't been there when she left in the morning. And by that time Simon's party had already sailed on *Sunbird*; she had found them moored on the Broad with chairs and drinks set out. Thus an alibi seemed to exist for the Lazy Waters party, and she was somewhat abashed by this exclusion of her principal suspects. But then she remembered: there was Woody. He hadn't been with them when she arrived. He had been out with the launch and had turned up an hour later.

But Woody . . . what reason would he have to interfere between herself and Keith? She would have thought him the least likely of that crowd to have behaved in such a manner. Could he be sweet on her himself? She didn't think it very probable; he seemed much too self-absorbed, in a way almost sexless. He had been friendly enough but that seemed part of his nature, and she was positive she would have noticed if there had been any more to it.

But then she reflected that his having opportunity didn't necessarily fix the letter on Woody. There was one other contender at least: Simon himself had been out in the launch. But here again, what could be the motive? The facts denied there was one. By word and deed Simon had encouraged her association with his nephew. He was been consistent in this from the outset, no less today than on other occasions, and if he had known that Dawn was in a plot against her then it was Dawn who would have received the warning. There was also the style of the letter, which was scarcely that of a practising writer. Stella felt that though Simon might have sought to disguise the style, he wouldn't be able to refrain from giving it punctuation. No; by the literary test, a likelier prospect was Sam Fulcher – and Fulcher did have motive, that of supposed injury, along with a mischief-making nature. She retrieved the letter and smoothed it out. But she saw it was written on an expensive bond; it had also, she now noticed, a strip torn from it, obviously to remove a printed address. And – if not Fulcher? She flung the letter down a second time and trampled it underfoot. Not George. She wouldn't have that. She would have sworn for George in a court of law.

Then she stood very still, recalling suddenly a tiny detail. That rub on the launch's varnish which she had noticed when Woody brought it in! It had been fresh, she was certain, she remembered the frown Simon had given it; and where had Woody been in the launch to get a rub like that? She knew the answer without thinking. He'd got it while mooring at the summerhouse. There was a bolt-head in the piling which she always avoided when mooring the dinghy. She stuck her feet into some sandals, threw a mac over her shoulders, and armed with a torch went hastening down the track to the summer-house. There she kneeled and directed the beam along the rough timber piles. She found the bolt-head: its rusty knob had a gouging of white on it. She touched it with her finger and brought away some powdered varnish: proof. Woody had been there and had pushed that letter through her door.

She remained kneeling for a while, unconscious of discomfort to her knees, her torch still playing on the silent witness she had found. Why, and again, why? Why choose this underhand method? If he knew of something aimed against her, why not come out with it to her face? Her anger, which had abated a little in the triumph of detection, now began to well back as she considered Woody's behaviour. There was an element so gra-tuitous in the insult the letter put on her, it had been totally unnecessary and yet so deliberately done. And it was a threat-ening sort of letter, far from being a 'friendly warning'; it sought to inspire her with fear of some consequence unnamed. Well, she would treat it exactly as it deserved. She would show him just how little she could be moved by such attempts at intimidation.

She rose, dusted her knees, and turned to set off back to the cottage. But then she heard, not far off, Keith's voice calling her name. She switched on her torch again and stood waiting at the staithe, and shortly she heard the splash of his swimming and he came oaring into the light.

'Keith. You can just turn round and swim straight back to *Sunbird*.'

'It's all right, Stella.' His hand reached up to grab the staithing near her feet. 'I was only out for a swim . . honestly. I thought you'd have gone to bed by now.'

'You weren't coming to the cottage?'

'No, honestly.'

'I don't want you swimming out this way, either.'

He looked curiously unlike himself as he hung there in the water, his hair flattened over his eyes, face dripping and moonlike. She realised with a little shock that he was perfectly naked and she felt the stirring of desire which the knowledge prompted. Damn Woody, damn all the race of snoopers and mischief-makers! Her defiance flamed silently over the dark reaches of the Broad. The flavour of last night lingered on her reawakened palate, reminding her that in love the second course was often the sweetest.

'You can stay.'

She stood back a pace, letting her mac fall partly open. She had been undressing when she found the letter and she was pretty well as stark as himself. She heard the quick-taken breath which he tried to subdue, and she laughed deep in her throat. Tonight, she thought, he was going to learn something.

In the morning she burned the letter. She made a little ritual of it, dousing it first in lighter-fuel to ensure a merry blaze. While it burned she went through the motions of wiping her hands over it – for Stella, there would always be a symbolic element in the burning of a manuscript.

It was raining that morning for the first time since she had arrived, but she had no outdoor plans and the murmur of rain was rather pleasant. Her single excursion was to the summer-house to put the dinghy under cover and to collect the towel which Keith had muddied and which now she put to soak. She did some other chores, though nothing requiring much energy. She smiled to herself at the weary feeling in her limbs. He had asked for it, that kid, and now he knew what it was he'd asked for. She wondered what he was thinking about his experiences of the night and she felt a moment of guilt: but ask for it he certainly had.

She was making herself a mug of coffee when Simon's car drew up. He knocked peremptorily, then let himself in before she could answer the door. He took a couple of steps into the room and glanced through into the kitchen before asking her, sharply:

'Keith is here with you, isn't he?'

'Keith . . . what do you mean?' She flushed indignantly, moving towards him. Good Lord, this was getting to be more than she could stomach!

'He's here in the cottage.'

'He is not. I haven't seen him.'

'My dear, I checked the summerhouse earlier. And he isn't at Lazy Waters.'

'And just why should he be here?'

Simon shrugged. 'Let's be frank, shall we? He isn't on *Sunbird*, but he swam down this way last night.'

She was appalled. So the swine had actually been keeping a tag on Keith – he had had the gall to spy on him when he went off on his swims! A fine kettle of fish she had got herself mixed up with – anonymous letters, espionage, and now downright persecution.

'So?' She spat the word.

'So?' Simon gestured. 'I want to know, my dear. Even if it's only to bring him his clothes.'

'Exactly how do his clothes come into it?'

'He wasn't wearing any when he left *Sunbird*.'

'How do *you* know he wasn't wearing any?'

'Because, my dear, they are still in his cabin.'

'Because you watched him!' She kept her distance; she was afraid she might strike him. Her whole being revolted at his smoothfaced hypocrisy. 'You watched him. You wanted to find out whether he was coming here or not. You're a scheming spy, Simon, and I'm not sure if you're not something worse.'

'My dear, let us keep our temper.' Simon's hand lifted placatingly. 'I admit that I watched Keith set off on his swim. Night-swimming is a foolish fad of his and I am not much in favour of it. Without being the heavy uncle, I like to know when he's out swimming.'

'And you know where he swam to.'

'There's no mystery about that. I enquired of Fulcher on my way down the Broad.'

'Fulcher! Then Fulcher is still one of your . . . creatures.'

'He was babbing for eels, my dear. He heard Keith swim past this way.'

It was pat, but Stella didn't believe him for a moment. So Fulcher was part of this conspiracy, an extra eye on the watch! She should have guessed it from the first, the fellow was always hanging about there: and hadn't he been in Simon's pay in the matter of the late Vanessa? Perhaps Woody had something to be said in his favour after all . . .

'And now you know, what about it?'

Simon shook his head. 'But I don't know. And if he really isn't here, then I'm afraid it's a little serious.'

'Serious? Why?'

'I should have thought that was obvious. It seems that Keith has disappeared. Unless you have something to add to the tale, Fulcher was the last person to have seen him.'

'But that . . . that's ridiculous!' Stella's flush was no longer entirely indignant. 'All right then, I did see him. He swam up to the summerhouse.'

'And spent the night there?'

'He did nothing of the sort!'

'Then where did he go?'

'He swam back to *Sunbird*.'

Simon continued to shake his head. 'No he didn't,' he replied. 'At least, he wasn't back there when I turned in at half-past twelve. You will forgive me for saying so, but I assumed that he was spending the night here, though since he departed in his birthday suit I supposed he would return early this morning. But he hasn't returned, and his bunk hasn't been slept in. And the clothes he came aboard in are still where he left them. So is his watch. And so is his wallet.'

Stella was silenced, a crevice of fear opening suddenly in her mind. If this were true . . . but no, one mustn't jump to conclusions! As far as she knew, Keith had set out intending to return to *Sunbird*. But he hadn't expressly declared an intention of doing that.

'You say you have been to Lazy Waters.'

'I took a look in his bedroom. Molly had seen nothing of him, but she would probably have been in bed.'

'Were any of his clothes missing from there?'

'I don't know that for certain. He could have made his own bed of course, though he's not in the habit of doing so. At what time did he set off back?'

'I'm not . . . sure. It might have been one, or a little later.'

'To come back to *Sunbird*?'

'He didn't actually say so.'

'He said nothing that might lead you to think otherwise.'

'No. He didn't.'

'Then perhaps you can appreciate my anxiety. As far as we know he set off to swim back, but failed to turn up at the other end.'

'But Simon . . . I can't believe it!' Stella's resentment had vanished now. The jagged edge of that fear was spreading wider and wider. 'He must have gone off somewhere else, he's a kid with the queerest ideas. He may have spent the night in one of the boats, or fetched some clothes and gone off on a hike . . .'

Simon's shoulders hunched feebly. 'I wish I could believe that, my dear.'

'But isn't it probable? I know him, I tell you. He's capable of any sort of freak.'

'Then where do you suggest we look for him?'

'About the boats . . . anywhere! There's an old yacht we looked at yesterday. And there's George. The man on the houseboat.'

'You mean the houseboat moored at the top here?'

'Yes. Yes! He'd have to pass it, wouldn't he?'

Simon nodded very thoughtfully. 'There's a chance there, I suppose.'

'Ask him, Simon. Ask everywhere.'

'My dear, that's what I'm doing.'

'He'll be around, I know he will. It's too fantastic . . . we've got to find him!'

She felt a sick panic take her and was conscious of a whiteness under her eyes. It wasn't true, couldn't be true: nothing serious could have happened to Keith. Some crazy fancy . . . that was his mark. A stunt to make people take notice. Not realising, of course, that anyone would worry about him – he hadn't been used to it: it wouldn't cross his mind.

'Simon, we've got to find him!'

She became aware of his arm around her shoulder.

'Take it easy, my dear. It could very well be as you say.'

'Simon, if anything has happened to him –'

'Then it'll be his own silly fault.'

'But he came down here to see me . . . if anything's happened, I'm to blame!'

She felt tears welling up and she flung away from Simon: she stood with her back to him, biting her lips, fighting the temptation to break into sobs. No, she kept telling herself, she wasn't going to cry on his chest. She wasn't going to cry at all. Not in the presence of Simon.

'Listen Stella. You have nothing to blame yourself for. Going swimming in the dark was something that Keith did in any case.'

'But it was me he came to see, Simon.'

'He could have taken a boat, couldn't he? He wasn't under a compulsion to swim when he went to visit you.'

'But . . .' She couldn't bring herself to say what was passing through her mind. She was thinking that after what had passed between them Keith's swimming could not have been at its strongest. At the time, noticing his tiredness, she had hinted that he should take her dinghy, but Keith apparently had viewed the suggestion as a reflection on his virility. Instead of slipping into the water he had done a flattish dive off the staithe.

'There are no "buts" about it, my dear. You can't fly in the face of facts. And in any case we are not sure yet that anything has happened to him. I'm going back to *Sunbird* now to see if the young fool has shown up, and on the way I shall make whatever enquiries I can. You wouldn't like to come along?'

She shook her head. 'No, Simon.'

'I wouldn't brood over it, my dear. It may be a false alarm after all.' He came round so that he was facing her and touched her gently on the shoulder. 'And I'm sorry, my dear. I didn't mean to be offensive.'

When he had gone she sank into a chair, her eyes fixed on the mug of cold coffee. She could think of only one thing. She'd been a bitch to the poor kid.

22

During the slow march of that rainy morning Stella twice rang
Lazy Waters, but on each occasion she was answered only by
Molly, Simon's cook-housekeeper. There was no word of Keith
nor any news of what Simon was doing, though she learned that
Sunbird had returned and that Simon had spent a long time on
the phone. After lunch, which was a farce of sardines and
biscuits, Stella made up her mind to do something herself. She
would take the dinghy and row across for a talk with George;
then she would visit the old yacht, about which she felt an
intuition. She put on her mac and went down to the mooring.
She found that the dinghy had taken some rain and would need
bailing out. She was just finishing this job when the creak of a
rowlock caught her ear and she saw, out in the channel, a sight
that made her heart stand still. They had the drags out. Two
double-ended boats, in one of which sat a uniformed policeman, were rowing slowly back and forth, each boat towing
something behind it. She dropped the bailer in the dinghy and
hastily scrambled ashore. She was very nearly sick. She walked
unsteadily back to the cottage.

It was only too clear now whom Simon had been telephoning
and what conclusion they had come to. Keith was missing and
presumed drowned: she had watched him swim away to his
death. Every time she thought about it the idea almost caused
her to retch. Out of her arms he had gone, faint from the passion
she had subjected him to – that was the worst part of it: her
demands on him had been so ruthless. She had killed him with
her libidinous and selfish desire, she was guilty of his death: she
had sinned and he had paid for it. In a turmoil of stunned
horror she paced up and down her small parlour. It wasn't even
as though what she had done had been the consequence of love

for him. She had never felt the least affection for him, he had been a plaything, a vanity. Her whole attitude to him had been selfish under a show of benevolence. She had made use of him to fill the gap which Justin had left in her self-esteem, a piece of weak and egoistic behaviour which in another she would have harshly condemned. And now she was reaping what she had sown. Her dragon's teeth were up with a vengeance.

The phone jangled; she snatched at it, then held it down on the rest for a moment. By being too hasty it seemed almost that she might precipitate bad news.

'Simon?'

'Yes, my dear . . . it's about Keith. They've found him.'

'Found him . . .?'

'They've just taken him out of the Broad, I'm afraid.'

'Oh God!'

'I thought I should let you know straight away, Stella. I've seen him . . . they are taking the body to Staybridge.'

She set her hip against the cabinet on which the phone stood, feeling the room slant towards her as though tilted on gimbals. She had known she was going to hear it ever since she had seen the dragging, yet falsely and treacherously she had still permitted herself to hope. And now there were no more grounds for hoping. The words had been spoken that would echo till eternity.

'He – he was drowned?' she got out, her voice sounding alien to her.

'Yes . . . ultimately.' Simon also sounded like a stranger. 'Someone collided with him, we think . . . there's a nasty bit of bruising. Quite a number of damned fools try to navigate after dark.'

'Then he didn't just . . . go under?'

'No. Not Keith. He's a distance man. I've just been explaining that to the constable. Keith was run down, it's the only answer.'

'Oh God, the poor kid.'

'At least he wouldn't have known much about it.'

'But what a thing to happen.'

'Yes. It was a stupid way to go.'

She struggled angrily with the relief that she couldn't help feeling, relief at the intelligence that she wasn't the agent of Keith's death. But it was plain from Simon's account that the blame lay elsewhere, and that at the time of the accident he was experiencing no difficulties. As she was human she couldn't help feeling thankful for that.

'There will be a PM of course, the police will insist on it. And I thought you would like to know that your name hasn't been mentioned. It seemed irrelevant, my dear, and you've had enough trouble. For the purpose of the inquiry it will be sufficient that Keith was swimming on the Broad.'

'But Simon –'

'Yes?'

'I don't know . . . don't you think I ought to?'

'Give testimony, you mean? You would be a fool to, Stella.'

'But surely they will want to know . . . ?'

'They will want to know how he died. And since you can't help them with that, you will do best to stay clear.'

It was easy to acquiesce. She hadn't thought about an inquiry, but now that she did she could see clearly that it might be extremely humiliating. It would be bad enough to have to undergo the questions of the local police and the coroner, but the testimony she had to give would add a dangerous pungency to the case. The Sunday papers might get hold of it. And they had photographs of Stella.

'If you didn't mention me, Simon –'

'Oh, I mentioned you, my dear. I told the constable that you were my tenant and that you had spent the day on *Sunbird*. At the most they may want your testimony on Keith's habit of taking moonlight dips, but even that's unlikely. All the rest of us knew about it.'

'I'll take your advice then.'

'It's the only wise course. Don't forget that we are most of us in the public eye a bit.'

'There's just the matter of the time . . .'

'My dear, leave that to the post mortem. It will give them all they want and perhaps nail the boat that did it.'

After he had rung off she remained for a long time leaning against the cabinet. Her mind was in a whirl and it refused to settle down. When the first numbing shock of the tragedy had worn away, the details of it, without logical sequence, kept churning through her brain. The poor kid, the poor kid! She couldn't ease her conscience completely. Because of her, it might be, he had been less alert, less prompt to act. That last moment effort that might have averted the accident . . . she found herself with her hand out, trying to fend the image from her. Oughtn't she to tell the police anyway, to pinpoint that moment? To give them something certain to start with in their search for the boat responsible? But no, the people aboard her had been simply puppets like herself, there was no point, no justice in bringing their unconscious deed home to them. It was a tragedy and a farce in which blame had no meaning. And Keith had died as a result of it. Wickedly. Cruelly. One could call on a god, but how could one believe in providence?

She was startled again by the ringing of the phone, but this time she swept it up with no preliminary, pacifying pause. At the other end there was a silence that lasted for some seconds, then a rough voice which she recognised said:

'Know who I am, Miss Stella?'

'Yes. What do you want?' She nearly slammed the phone down. It was Fulcher, and she was astounded at his impertinence in ringing her up.

'Now don't you get upshus when I only want to be friendly. There's no call for that, none at all, Miss Stella.'

'What do you want?' She made no attempt to hide the scorn she felt for him.

'I'll tell you, my girl. That's just a friendly little hint.'

It was the slight edge of menace that made her hesitate to cut him off: she listened, her fingers hovering over the studs.

'Now this little bit of trouble what's cropped up lately . . . you know where I am? But I daresay you do. Well, I reckon that'd be best if you kept your oar out. That's plain enough, isn't it? You keep your oar out.'

'Thanks,'she replied icily. 'But your master has already told me.'

'My what?'

'Your master. Mr Lea-Stephens.'

'Oh-ah.' The fellow seemed put out by this rejoinder. 'Well, now I'm telling you too, so's there won't be no mistake.'

'And that's *all* you have to tell me?'

'That's all for just now –'

'Good day, Mr Fulcher. And don't bother to ring again.'

He was still saying something when she pressed down on the studs. She felt beyond being angry, she had only a fleeting contempt for him. But she didn't much like the conspiratorial flavour of the business, the apparent determination of everyone to dissuade her from giving testimony. Of course, she thought wearily, Fulcher had guessed where Keith was off to, he had kept an eye on the pair of them for the last day or two. It was a comfort that he had been briefed to keep the affair to himself, but she would never forgive Simon for setting the fellow to spy on them. Why had he done it, in any case – why had he taken this perverse interest? He had practically fathered the affair and then, as it developed . . .

Her mind fetched up short as she saw suddenly where her thoughts were tending. Good God . . . she mustn't start getting ideas of that sort! She was overwrought, she had better be careful what she was thinking, it was the curse of her profession to have a riotous imagination. But Simon *had* almost driven her into opening her arms to Keith, he *had* spied on their meetings, he *had* . . . she paused. Didn't he have a motive too?

Fiercely she told herself: 'Stella Rushton, get up and do something!' – and she seized a feather duster and began furiously to go round the room. It was bad enough, ugly enough, it didn't need her lurid suspicions. Simon was deep and possibly treacherous, but it was absurd to imagine him anything worse.

23

The rain cleared away during the afternoon to leave a mild, scented evening. Stella, restless in her agitation, walked down to the summerhouse again. Several times she had had the feeling, it had come almost like a panic, that her only sensible course was to pack her bags and get away. Her solitude had become a burden, she felt that now she could never bear it. To go on living there after what had happened was a prospect that filled her with dismay. She longed to draw a curtain over it, to erase the image from her brain: she needed London, gay people: anything to stop her agonised brooding.

She climbed the steps to the summerhouse as a deliberate act of penance. It was such a short time ago that she had led Keith up there. This was still the day after the night, no second darkness had intervened, the floor was still a little damp where he had stood and towelled himself. Was it real, what had happened? Her brain felt dizzy and overwhelmed. His death seemed so improbable in that mute and unchanged room. The cushions lay there where they had left them, bearing the imprint of their bodies, and her limbs were full of the tiredness which their lovemaking had evoked. But he, he felt none of that, he neither felt nor thought. There was yet a Broad, yet a *Lutestring*, but his part in them had lapsed. And all the emotion and fear and striving that had been for her, that was cured in a moment, it didn't trouble Keith now. And still everything continued in just the way it had been. Nothing took the slightest notice of his abrupt withdrawal from the scene. All that which had delighted him and made the world he took for granted, it went on its way without him, taken for granted by the living. How did it happen that a human personality was so casually extinguished, what was there important in man's affairs, in the light of this?

And he was dead; yet, she thought, for her he had never been more alive. She felt much more conscious of his presence than she had ever done while he was with her. Only now he seemed to be smiling, as though in his great release from passion, as though he had found a wondrous answer and was sunnily in peace. So strong did this feeling become that she wondered if he really were present, his spirit still lingering there in the place where they had been together. She felt the tears stinging her eyes; it was true that she had been a bitch to him. She had nothing to offer but her remorse to his returning, compassionate ghost. She hoped that he understood that being human, she was weak and selfish. She was still a novice in life while he had attained the wisdom of death.

From these thoughts she was roused by the sound of oars on the water below and she went across to the veranda to see who was disturbing her privacy. It was George, rowing his dinghy, and she viewed his arrival with mixed feelings. But she went slowly down the steps to see what he wanted. He saw her and rested his oars.

'Hullo there! Mind my calling on you?'

Stella briefly shook her head. She stooped to take the dinghy's painter. George shipped his oars and stepped firmly from the dinghy; he had the unfussiness of a big man who was familiar with small boats.

'I was down in the village shopping when I heard about the accident. Thought I would row across and offer you my sympathies.'

'That was kind of you, George.'

'I had seen you sailing with the young man.'

'Yes . . . we were friends.'

'Mmn. It's a sad business.'

He looked about for somewhere to sit, pitching finally on a mooring post; then he made quite a business of filling and lighting his pipe. She watched him, grateful for this interval of silence.

'Had you known him long?'

'No, I'd only just met him – a day or two ago. He came down with Simon.'

'He looked like a young man who might throw his heart at someone.'

She smiled faintly. 'He was. He threw it at me.'

George puffed. 'Was he welcome?'

'I don't know,' she sighed. 'He was a mixed-up young man. You felt you wanted to help him. But I'm not the sort, really, it calls for an angel or something. I tried. Or I didn't try. That's what makes it so beastly.'

'You had better blame yourself. It's the natural reaction.'

'I'm doing it, anyway.'

'When someone dies there is a general tendency to feel guilty. When there isn't, watch out. You may find something else.'

'I keep forgetting you're one of the profession.'

He rocked his shoulders and grinned at her from behind the pipe.

'But you'll know Lea-Stephens pretty well – you being another writer?'

'Simon?' She shook her head, thinking how little she really knew about him. 'I met him a week or two ago when I rented the cottage. Oh and once before, at a party. So I can't claim a long acquaintance.'

'Someone suggested the cottage, did they?'

'Yes. A mutual friend.'

'Was he sticky about letting it?'

'Oh no. Not a bit. I was feeling rather . . .' She broke off, Justin looming on her horizon. She glanced quickly at George, half-questioning, half-appealing.

'I see the gossip columns,' he said simply. 'I couldn't help knowing about you, Stella.'

She nodded, her gaze falling. 'I don't want to talk about that. It seems so petty and frivolous now. But at the time it meant something and I wanted to get away from it, and Simon was very nice about the cottage. The rent he charges is ridiculous.'

'How do you get on with his friends?'

'Oh . . .!' It was her turn to rock her shoulders. 'They're theatre types, George, if you know what that means.'

'Mmn. I think I do. And how did your young man get on with them?'

'Keith was completely out of it. Which is probably why he turned to me.'

George continued to puff in the placid way he had, his greenish eyes looking dreamy through the wreaths of smoke. It was soothing Stella to talk and he was tossing her all the openings: intentionally, she was sure, in his best bedside manner.

'He was an orphan, wasn't he? I heard it mentioned in the shop.'

'Yes. At least, his father was dead. He told me his mother had been divorced.'

'He lived with his grandfather, they say.'

'The grandfather is Lea-Stephens Engineering. Keith was booked to go into the firm when he came down from Cambridge. He wasn't keen, poor boy. He felt he wasn't engineering-minded. I think his heart was in boats . . . not that it matters now.'

'It will be a blow for his grandfather.'

Stella felt a little hot. She remembered her wild supposition that George had been Keith's grandfather in disguise. 'I'm afraid that Simon will have a harrowing time when he meets his father . . . quite apart from anything else, his father didn't know that Keith was down here.'

'Didn't know.?'

Now she blushed. She knew she ought not to have mentioned it. 'Well, there is some silly row between Simon and his father. Keith was keen to come down here, but he knew that his grandfather would disapprove, so Simon suggested he tell the old boy that he was staying with college friends. But please, that's confidential. I shouldn't have told it to anyone.'

George nodded seriously. 'He was a foolish young man.'

'Yes he was. But most young men are foolish.'

'It's their privilege . . . we daren't be foolish after thirty.'

'Make it thirty-two, George. I'm still a foolish woman my-self.'

She looked about as he had done and found that the posts were the only furniture, so she squatted on the one next to his with as much dignity as she could muster. She might well have asked him up to the superior comfort of the summerhouse, but she felt a certain reluctance to introducing him there. And he appeared quite comfortable on a post.

'Who is this Dawn le Fay person I hear about?'

'*Née* Molly Jimpson.' Stella contrived to pull a face. 'She's an actress who had a part in Simon's musical. An overloaded blonde. You'd probably find her a drag.'

'Is there anyone else staying there I should have heard of?'

'There's Woody. Woody Woodmancott. He writes the music.'

'Who is Glynda?'

She shot him a look. 'You have heard about Glynda?'

'Mmn.' He inclined his head. 'They have a good grapevine in Alderford.'

'Well . . . she's Simon's girlfriend. A rep actress who's resting. I think she's likely to get the push – Simon finds engagements for his ex's.'

'It sounds an interesting household.'

'It isn't really. It's dull. Then there's a set-designer, Jeff Simpson, and Jill, Simon's secretary. That's all.'

'And Keith didn't take much to this assembly.'

'He didn't take to it at all.'

'And what were their reactions to him?'

'I don't think they much noticed him. Dawn did, of course, but she was poison to poor Keith. She was a bit put out when he favoured me. I think she regarded him as her private property.'

'How do you mean?'

Once more Stella's tongue had strayed a little, and she found it exceedingly difficult to retrieve a false step. She gave a hesitant shrug, her eyes straying away from George. But then she thought: to hell with Simon. What loyalty did she owe him and his crowd?

'This is gossip, you understand. I wouldn't want it to go further.'

George nodded in his solemn and confidential manner. She told him briefly of Glynda's jealousy and the petty intrigues it gave rise to, of Simon's machiavellian shifts to preserve a quiet life. She found the subject oddly distasteful: it sounded particularly trivial and ugly. George listened without expression, puffing regularly on his pipe.

'So you practically had the young man forced on you?'

She stirred uncomfortably. 'I suppose I did. But Simon wasn't quite so cynical, he thought it would give me an interest. I was feeling very upset when I came down here.'

'Mmn. On the rebound.'

'That's not very kind, George.'

'It was true though, wasn't it? And he could scarcely not have known.'

'I think you're being unfair to Simon.'

George smoked away silently. He seemed to retreat into his meditations, his eyes becoming remote from Stella. He had injected a note of brusqueness into his last few remarks, and she was not at all certain that she didn't feel hurt by it.

'The cottage. What did you know about that when you hired it?'

Stella was startled by the abruptness and harsh tone of the enquiry.

'Simon gave me a description of it.'

'Did he tell you it was a love-nest?'

'Well, really!' She sat up straighter. 'And what do *you* know about it, anyway?'

'It's common knowledge. He didn't tell you?'

'No. When I found out I was angry with him.'

'How did you find out?'

'I –' Stella checked herself quickly. 'That's my business, George. And I don't like being interrogated.'

Still there was no expression on his placid, square-jawed face, nor any variation in the slow rhythm of his puffs. She felt her resentment begin to gather. She had been too hasty in trusting this man! He was pumping her, that was it, and she had only just begun to cotton on.

'Perhaps I should tell you, then, what they're saying in the village.'

'No.' She rose. 'I don't want to hear it, George.'

'Sit down. I think you should hear it.'

'I won't listen to village gossip!'

'I'd like to know if there is any truth in what passes for gospel down there.'

'Very well then.' She breathed deeply and resumed her squat on the post. 'But I'm telling you George, this is none of your business. I thought you came here to be kind and to sympathise with me, but I don't much care for the way you're going about it.'

He ignored her little outburst. 'It amounts to this, Stella. There's a certain party, a bit unpopular, who used to be welcomed at the cottage, and who at one time or another has been in the pay of Mr Simon. Now I hear that this party tried to re-establish himself, but that he met with a rebuff. Would that be true, or wouldn't it?'

She was flaming. 'Yes, it's true. Now I hope you're satisfied!'

He heaved his large shoulders. 'Just puzzled,' he said.

'And who asked you to be puzzled?'

'Listen.' He raised his hand suddenly. 'I wonder if you recognise something we can hear?'

She stared at him angrily, half expecting a trick, then turned her attention perfunctorily to the evening sounds of the Broad. She heard the usual chitter of the reed birds, the croon of a pigeon in the carrs, and the reel of a grasshopper-warbler coming from reeds close to the mooring.

'What am I supposed to be listening for?'

'Do you know the sound of a diesel engine?'

She heard it then. It was the persistent throbbing note of Simon's launch.

'And what about it?'

'It's distinctive, isn't it?'

'Suppose it is. What then?'

'Just that I heard it last night. At around one o'clock-time.'

24

For some moments she felt unable to stir or utter a word. She sat rigidly on the post, her breathing limited to checked gasps. The implication of what he said opened a vein of sapping fear, jerking to life as it did the faint suspicion she had toyed with earlier. Simon: Simon had been there. And at the critical time, near enough. At the most, within half-an-hour of when Keith had set out. And he had said nothing about it, he had told her he'd gone to bed – a lie, a palpable lie! For he had been out on the Broad. The fear of it swept through her like a deadly contagion and she snatched at the first hint of doubt she could muster.

'But . . . how can you be certain?'

George slowly shook his head at her. 'I can't be. Not if you mean about whose engine I heard. I can only say I heard an engine that sounded identical with one I know, and that's poorish sort of evidence to give in a court of law.'

'Yes.' She felt a rush of relief. 'Yes, it might not have been Simon.'

'It might not. There must be other boats with engines like that. And then, we don't know at what time the accident happened. We would have to know it fairly closely to jump to a conclusion . . . wouldn't we?'

He knew. She snatched out her cigarettes in a desperate attempt to cover her confusion. She had made him a present of the vital fact that she was aware of the time, and when it was. She didn't know if he had deliberately set a trap to catch her, but she had given herself away – and George was not the man to miss it. She fumbled a fag into her mouth, and lit it.

'You . . . you'd better tell the police.'

'I'm not so sure of that yet.' He took the lighted match from her and applied it to his pipe.

'It's important. They had better know.'

'I wonder if it is important?'

'It is. And you know it. So you'd better go and tell them.'

'Mmn.' He let the match drop to fizz in the water. 'I don't like being precipitate when it comes to police matters. You shove something under their noses and it can make a lot of trouble . . . for them, as well as other people. And there may be nothing in it.'

She shivered. She watched the cigarette in her hand trembling helplessly. It was possible: she might be agitating herself over nothing. It might have been some other boat, Simon could simply have been spying, he might well have returned to *Sunbird* before Keith came on the scene. Swimming slowly, as he would have done, Keith might have arrived at the spot considerably later.

'Tell me about . . . what you heard.'

'Yes.' George shaped a ring. 'Well, I packed in fishing at eleven, then I made some coffee and lay reading on my bunk. It was pretty quiet outside. I could hear a fish or two rising, and something' – he paused – 'which could have been an otter. Then, towards one, I scraped out my pipe and turned out the light, and lay a few minutes thinking about one thing or another. And it was just a little later that I heard the engine. But it meant nothing to me, and I simply went off to sleep.'

'So you could have dreamed it, about the engine.'

'No Stella, I'm afraid I couldn't. I heard it plainly enough – over there, in the channel.'

'And it was about one . . . you're sure of the time?'

He held her eyes. 'It's important, isn't it?'

'Yes,' she breathed. 'Yes, it is.'

'Well . . . it would be only a few minutes afterwards.'

She drew heavily on her cigarette, trying to reassure herself with this. Simon was a liar, but it didn't follow that he was a murderer as well. He wasn't the type, she told herself, imagining his falsely-frank eyes; he liked finesse, he was an intriguer, violence didn't form part of his character. It was much more likely that he came out to spy than with the intention of running Keith down. He had scarcely hidden his curiosity to find out what her relations were with Keith.

'You think I would be wise to keep quiet for a bit?'

George had risen; he was stretching himself and tapping out his pipe.

'It's . . . well, it's up to you.' Stella refused to give him the satisfaction of being asked for his silence.

'Mmn. In that case I won't be in a hurry . . . I'll just wait, and watch events.' He came closer. 'And I really am sorry. You've been taking it on the chin lately. Let me prescribe an early night for you. And some hot whisky, and three aspirins.'

'Thank you, doctor. That's a good idea.'

'And stop wallowing in the blame. It's a commonplace reaction and it won't alter a thing.'

It was superfluous enough, that parting admonition. Stella had been shaken out of any tendency to continue her wallowing. Something else had replaced it, an emotion much more powerful and exclusive, and though she could meet it with self-assurances it was a long way from being stilled. She walked briskly back to the cottage where she followed George's prescription to the letter. She wasn't very fond of whisky so she added several spoonfuls of sugar to it. Then she took care to check the bolts, a precaution she sometimes forgot, and made a round of the windows before retiring to her room. It was a jolt, a terrible jolt: she wouldn't believe it, but she couldn't forget it. Though she drank the whisky in greedy mouthfuls it seemed to be neutralised by the fear in her stomach.

For didn't Simon have sufficient motive, when you began to review the circumstances? George obviously had suspected it and had come probing her for information. For that was what he had done, she had no illusions about that; using his casual, practitioner's technique he had got her to sketch in the outline for him. And the outline threw it up plainly: Keith had stood in Simon's way. Keith was the old man's favourite, Simon the black sheep of the family. And there would be a lot of money in it, all the wealth of Lea-Stephens Engineering. Stella didn't know how much that was but she did know that the firm was one of the large ones. It was a motive as cogent as any could be – in spite of Simon himself being passing rich.

She shuddered, she sucked the last of the whisky from the glass. It was supposition only! There was no shadow of proof to underwrite it. And for all she knew Simon's inheritance was established and certain, and the rows he had with his father as insignificant as summer showers. No, if one began looking at motives any accident could be suspect, there was positively no limit to what the imagination might invent; and when you came to it, George had heard but he hadn't seen the launch: five other people besides Simon had been on *Sunbird* the previous night.

Immediately she found herself extending her volatile suspicions. Woody! His was the name that jumped at once into her mind. Woody, with his anonymous warning, his cryptic remark, his use of the launch – she didn't try to guess at his motive: for an accusing moment her conviction ignored it. And Woody, he was the type, the subhuman, expressionless egotist, hiding his thoughts and feelings behind an affectation of indolence. She was convinced! But then her certainty ebbed away again. Of what was she convinced, except the fear that blinded her reason? Why not suppose Dawn a murderer, or Glynda, or Jeff Simpson – Jill, the perfect secretary, or Ruby, the perfect maid? They had all had an opportunity equal to Woody's, and were similarly unprovided with an adequate motive . . .

It was useless. There was no point in casting suspicion about in that way. She cursed George, who had plunged her into this ugly state of panic. A single, perhaps irrelevant fact, and the world assumed a nightmare quality, with monsters substituting themselves for fellow men and women. It was too much to credit, she would sooner discount the fact. Though George had been so cocksure he might easily have dreamed the sound of the engine. She toyed angrily with the idea that it had been a lie in the first place, but she was obliged to drop this notion when she remembered the time he had given. That was close, too close. He would have to have been a very lucky liar.

Finally his prescription did its work and she fell into a tossing, dreaming slumber. She started awake several times to find sweat on her forehead. In her dream, which was repetitive, she was sailing *Lutestring* with Keith; he kept asking reproachfully for the helm but every time she snubbed him to silence.

25

She woke with the comforting feeling that her fears too were dreamlike, and as easily to be banished by the bright morning sun. They did seem a little exaggerated as she reviewed them while dressing: the product of a mind unsettled by grief, not to be taken too seriously. She made a sagacious resolution: she would leave matters like that to the proper authorities. If there was anything suspect about Keith's accident it would undoubtedly come to their attention. They were better placed than herself to make an unprejudiced appraisal, and what was more they could test their suspicions instead of weighing one against the other. The latter was Stella's only method. She was glad to recognise its limitations.

Unfortunately she was not permitted to enjoy her tranquillity for long. The phone rang.

'Stella? My dear, you're wanted at the house.'

'Wanted? What for, Simon?'

'Oh, some damn silly questioning. They're making quite an issue of it. We have an inspector here now.'

'An inspector!'

'And a sergeant. And a female who scraps it all down. If you can be ready I'll pick you up in half an hour.'

'I . . . yes, all right, Simon.'

'That's time enough, is it?'

'Oh yes. I'll be ready.'

'Stiff uppers, my dear.'

An inspector . . . ! She took a step towards the door, then came to a stand. So there was something in it – the authorities *weren't* satisfied. Her panic fear came sweeping back, sapping her body with nausea. It had been murder: she was sure of that. Simon . . . somebody had murdered Keith. And she had been used . . . her attraction for Keith . . . she had been the bait in the trap set for him. How could she face Simon . . . anyone there? The police, the questions . . . ?

For some terrible minutes she wanted to run from the situation, and had a car been at her disposal she would most likely have fled. It was only by slow degrees that her mind began to clear again and the compulsion slackened in her pounding brain. She forced herself to go to the cabinet and pour a tot of brandy. Then, with as much assurance as she could muster, she lit a cigarette. Of course, she might be wrong; it needn't be as bad as she was imagining. She knew little or nothing of police procedure, this might all be a matter of course.

Simon's Jaguar arrived punctually. He came sweeping into the cottage. On his shapely features was a bad-tempered scowl.

'Damn them, I'm going to complain to someone. It's a blasted inquisition. From the way they carry on you would think I was harbouring a bunch of criminals.'

'What do they want to know, Simon?'

'Everything. When we last used the john. They've got a hang-up about Keith – they're sweating on promotion, it wouldn't surprise me.'

'But there must be something . . . special?'

'Oh, there is. At least, they pretend so. They've got a report from their futile pathologist. He thinks that Keith was bonked on the head.'

'You mean . . .?'

'Bonked. It's the only word for it. Not hit by a boat, that's far too simple. And so we all have to go through the wringer to see if their highnesses can spot a bonker.'

He went to Stella's cabinet and poured himself a drink, apparently unconscious of the effect of his words on her. On second thoughts he poured another and carried it to Stella. Her white face and shaking hand seemed for an instant to surprise him. Then his scowl faded slightly.

'Oh blast, Stella, I'm sorry . . . I'm upset myself, I don't know what I'm doing.'

'It's – it's horrible, Simon.'

'I know. And I don't believe it for a moment.'

'But if they say . . .'

He laughed angrily. 'How can they be sure, about a thing like that? The answer is they can't.'

'But they must . . . there must be something.'

'Oh certainly. There's promotion. So they're just trying it on.'

He threw back his drink and immediately went to pour himself another: he drank this one also in a couple of quick jerks. In the height of her agitation Stella was obliged to notice Simon's own. It was so unlike him. The mere perception of it added a cruel weight to her terrors. When she spoke her voice sounded thin, as though it had risen by an octave.

'Simon . . . I don't think I can see them just now.'

'What? Oh, my dear!' He came to drop on a chair beside her. 'But it's all right for you, you know, that's one blessing about it. We agreed to keep our mouths shut, and keep 'em shut we did.'

'But I shall have to tell them.'

'Tell them? Not you.'

'I will, Simon . . . it's different now. It isn't an accident any longer.'

'It was an accident, take my word for it. They are only trying the other for size. I saw the poor kid myself and they haven't a damned thing to go on. And if it wasn't an accident, my dear, you'd be the bigger idiot to get mixed up with it. Especially now, when we are all keeping quiet about you in our statements.'

'But it could be important.'

Simon shook his head vigorously. 'No more now than before, rest easy about that. The big question is still not *why* Keith went swimming, but who met him there, if they did, and what their object was in bonking him. And they fancy us for the job, I fear, individually or in concert. Which is only too plain from their way of going about it. Let me get you another drink.'

She accepted it unresistingly. She felt an increasing inability to oppose his will with hers. At first to make a clean breast had seemed the only path open to her, but she had little stomach to persist in it against the flow of his reasoning. Beside his strength she felt weak; she was ready enough to be persuaded.

'You see,' he seated himself again, 'it would look particularly odd now, giving them a piece of information which the rest of us have suppressed. It isn't important in itself but because it was suppressed they would think it was, and they would go over it with a microscope trying to make something of it. Then you can imagine what it would be like – hours and hours of blasted questioning. And all to no purpose as far as anything useful goes.'

'But if there was just a chance . . .'

'Then I would be all for it, Stella. I would be raising Cain, I can tell you, if I thought Keith had really been bonked. Damn it all, he *was* my nephew, and I was rather fond of the silly ass. It has been a hellish bit of business. I'm not a bloody lump of rock.'

'I didn't mean that, Simon.'

'I've got the dirty end of the stick. When they have kindly done with the body . . . and my father. It will hit him hard.'

She hesitated, then said: 'Doesn't he know about it yet?'

Simon shook his head. 'He may do. I sent off a cable yesterday.'

'A cable?'

'At this time of the year he's down at Juan les Pins. But he goes cruising with his pals and it isn't easy to contact him.'

'I see.' She bit her tongue to stop herself adding: 'How convenient.' She felt a compulsive urge to blurt out what George had told her about hearing the engine. Wouldn't it settle, once and for all, her paralysing suspicions concerning Simon – provoke, then and there, the moment of truth in his grey eyes? But she shuddered away from such a disclosure. Instead she made a final show of resistance.

'If they knew . . . about Keith and me . . . mightn't it help them find out who did it?'

Simon sighed. 'Very well then. If you've made up your mind to talk. But you will regret it, I think, and I'm certain that we shall. I ought to tell you that a reporter from the local is haunting Iriston.'

'Oh.'

'I wish you would think carefully before deciding to blow the gaff.'

She had expected him to be more energetic than this, but now he seemed to have grown tired of trying to cajole her into line. He remained silent for a space. Then he finished his drink.

'We had better be off my dear, or the Gestapo will get suspicious.'

She entered Lazy Waters that morning with the sensations of one entering a dental surgery, despairingly certain that at some juncture she would either faint or be sick; and as in the latter she had to wait, with her nerves growing less and less controllable, while other white-faced patients returned from the torture chamber. Simon sat her in the lounge along with Dawn and Glynda but beyond the bare civilities she felt unable to talk to them. Dawn, she noticed, wore a two-piece suit that might almost have been described as severe, while Glynda wore a drab-coloured dress with a chaste neckline and a low-cut hem. Neither was wearing much make-up. It was the day of the vicar's daughter.

When Stella arrived Woody had been the occupant of the hot-seat, but after quarter of an hour he emerged, looking more woeful than ever. He rolled his eyes at Dawn: 'You're next for the tumbril,' and seemed about to retire when his eye met Stella's. He hovered undecidedly. Then he shambled across to her. Stella rose and went out on the veranda and Woody hesitantly followed.

'It's hard lines, girlo . . . very hard lines.'

She kept her back to him. She said: 'You're rather clumsy with a launch, Woody.' As soon as the words were out she realised that he could put a wrong interpretation on them, but then it was too late. She grasped the veranda rail tightly.

'Yeah.' He purred the word. 'I'm not a mucher with those things, am I?'

'You should put out plenty of fenders when you moor at a quay-heading.'

'Yeah, I should, shouldn't I?'

'Otherwise you'll scratch the varnish.'

'I can see that, too.'

'And leave traces there for people to find.'

From the corner of her eye she saw his large hands close over the rail, more relaxed than her own and without the telltale white knuckles. She waited for him to reply but he leaned there silently. In a lower voice she added:

'Nothing could excuse that letter, Woody.'

'Yeah.' He hesitated again, pulling a little on his hands. Then: 'That's not quite true, girlo. There are some things could excuse it.'

'Such as?'

'Well, just some things.'

'I want to know what they are.'

'It wouldn't help a bit, girlo. That's all water under the bridge.'

'I think you owe me an explanation.'

'Yeah, maybe I do, too. But the way things have panned out . . . girlo, just let it ride.'

'If it's to do with Keith . . .'

She stopped, a new idea springing into her mind. Until now she had given no thought to the possible significance of that anonymous warning. But of what could Woody have been warning her if it were not of what had actually happened . . . giving proof, proof positive, that Keith's death had been contrived? She leaned forwards, an ominous dizziness seething up in her head. The stone flags of the path beneath her appeared to lift and ripple like the leaves of waterlilies. It would have been proof, but she had burnt it: perhaps the only proof that Keith was murdered. With her own hands she had destroyed the single, damning piece of evidence.

'It is . . . and it isn't.' She heard his slow voice beside her.

'Woody . . .'

'Take it easy, girlo. It wasn't to do with what you're thinking.'

'But if . . . if you knew . . .'

'I didn't know a darned thing. It was something else, something different. And now it doesn't matter a spit.'

She daren't press him. She felt obliged to accept the assurance he gave her. She couldn't bear a further evasion about the subject of the letter. Yes, it was probably innocent, probably referred to some intrigue of Dawn's; that was likely, more than likely. Simon himself had given her a hint of it. She drew deliberate, deep breaths, keeping her head leaned far forward, and after some moments the paving flags became stationary and level again.

'It's nerves, girlo, nerves. We've all got ourselves a dose of them. Once you start people going they'll believe the moon's a balloon. Like Othello and the hankie . . . which isn't so far-fetched, either. It's the kid having bought it that makes bogies out of bushes.'

'I'm feeling rather faint, Woody . . .'

'Yeah. I can see you are.'

'I think I'll sit down again.'

'I'll go fetch you a reviver.'

It was her fifth that morning but she drank it without a qualm. Usually it needed only two to give her a sensation of frivolity. Woody retired to the piano. He began playing his mindless music. She tried to fit her own mind to it, to make her brain just as empty and without purpose, but she found it hard not to be reminded that it was in this room she had met Keith. Woody had played his music then, at what seemed half a lifetime ago. Yet it was a matter of days, of hours: she could almost reach out and touch that evening.

Her summons came at last and it was Simon himself who fetched her. He tried to flash her one of his smiles but he couldn't hide the concern in his eyes. At the door of the study where the policemen were installed he gave her an encouraging pat on the shoulder, then held a finger to his lips. A moment later she was in the room.

26

'Take a chair, Miss Rushton.'

There were three policemen facing her. In front of the window had been placed a table, behind which two of them were seated. They were dressed in plain clothes and the one who had spoken had removed his jacket; he was a large fleshy man with faded fair hair and a squashed nose. His colleague looked rather younger and wore his hair down to his collar, and though they bore nothing to distinguish them one could tell at a glance that they were policemen. Both had watchful, examining stares, and an air of carefully observed restraint; like a pair of obedient gundogs eyeing a bird they might not yet seize. The third, a WPC in uniform, was sitting at a table to the side. Her tunic was unbuttoned, her cap and gloves lying in front of her. She was armed with a reporter's notebook and was sharpening a pencil with a razor-blade, and she hadn't bothered to look up as Stella came through the door. Stella sat on the chair placed for her. It was directly in front of the table.

'What is your permanent address, Miss Rushton?'

She gave it, and her other details. They were scribbled down by the WPC at a pace that seemed to devour Stella's words as she spoke them. The window was only slightly ajar. The atmosphere was hazy with smoke. The younger detective had been smoking but now he stubbed his cigarette; then he folded his arms and let the lids droop over his eyes. It was the elder man who was addressing her and he made a little speech.

'As I expect you know, Miss Rushton, we are investigating the death of Keith Lea-Stephens. We have asked you here because we think you can help our enquiries. It may be painful for you, I'm afraid, since I understand he was a friend of yours, but you will appreciate that we want to clear the matter up as quickly as possible.'

Stella nodded. She wished he wouldn't talk quite so fast. Her mind seemed sluggish and dragging and needed more time to comprehend him. The brilliant light from the window was coming from directly behind his head; it was a strain to focus her eyes on him, it gave her a sensation of remoteness.

'Did you know Keith Lea-Stephens before you met him in this house?'

'No . . . I didn't know him.' The pencil scribbled like a whispered echo.

'Had he been mentioned to you?'

'No.'

'He admired your writing I believe?'

'He said he did. I don't know. He had some books, books of mine.'

'I see.' The fleshy man, who was obviously the inspector in charge, looked frowningly at one of several typewritten sheets which lay on the table. 'You must have had plenty of opportunity to notice his relations with other people here. Did anything strike you in particular – anything you feel might have a bearing?'

This was much too complicated. Her mind struggled with it in dismay. It was as though she had ceased to be an intelligent person and had lapsed into idiocy. Her cheeks became hot.

'I don't understand . . . quite . . .'

'Miss Rushton, you will surely have been told that there is some doubt in this matter. To be frank, we are not certain that Keith Lea-Stephen's death was an accident. Now, I'm certain you will want to help us throw a little light on it.'

'Yes . . . yes. I do.'

'Then if you will just cast your mind back.'

'I'm trying . . . I can't remember. There was nothing that stands out.'

'Was he friendly with his uncle?'

'Oh yes. Quite friendly.'

'With Miss le Fay? Mr Woodmancott?'

'Yes. Everyone. They all liked him.'

'Was he particularly friendly with someone – apart from yourself, of course?'

'No, you see . . . he was different from them . . . he was a bit on his own.'

'Was Miss le Fay particularly friendly?'

'I . . . it's hard to explain.'

'Please try, Miss Rushton.'

'Yes. It's just that . . . well, they are all theatre people. He was an outsider, he didn't fit in. He wasn't used to that sort of person . . . but they weren't unkind to him.'

'And he had no particular friend – until you came along?'

She felt her cheeks growing hotter still. 'I didn't claim to be his particular friend.'

The inspector referred to his sheet. 'You went sailing with him once or twice?'

'Twice . . . yes.'

'You were the only person to do so.'

'Does that make me a particular friend?'

He gave her a penetrating stare but didn't pursue the point further. His younger colleague looked bored; he had his eyes fixed on the ceiling. A separate person from Stella was thinking: this is their everyday business, they will forget it over lunch, they'll talk of cricket or cars or something . . .

'I would like you to recall any conversation you remember, especially those that took place while Keith Lea-Stephens was absent. Can you remember what was said about him?'

'In what way . . . how do you mean?'

'Touching his relations with other people.'

'I don't . . . nothing was said . . .'

'Come now, Miss Rushton.'

She searched frenziedly in her memory for something harmless to give the brute, but her mind was almost a blank and she found it impossible to invent anything. Then she remembered a remark of Simon's.

'Mr Lea-Stephens thought it was good for him . . . mixing

with unusual people, I mean. He thought Keith needed drawing out a little.'

'He said that to you?'

'Yes . . . we were talking about Keith.'

'And that was perhaps his object in inviting his nephew to stay with him?'

'I don't know. It could have been.'

'To make him acquainted with some unusual people?'

'He didn't say that . . . Keith wanted to come. He was very keen on the Broads.'

'What else did Mr Lea-Stephens say?'

'Nothing. That's all I can remember.'

'Take your time, Miss Rushton.'

'It's no use. I can't remember.'

Again he transfixed her with his stare and she was certain he knew she was lying. It was a negative form of untruth, perhaps, but even this she was bad at. Her lips had gone dry, her mouth was nearly devoid of moisture; she could hear a pulse in her head as she waited for the next attack.

'You know Mr Simpson, of course?'

'Jeff Simpson. Yes.'

'Isn't he fond of Miss le Fay?'

She was surprised. 'Yes, I believe he is.'

'He is in love with her, in fact?'

'I . . . well, I couldn't say.'

'But he gave you that impression?'

'I suppose he did. He's very fond of her.'

'Now think carefully, Miss Rushton. What was Miss le Fay's attitude to the deceased?'

'She was . . .' Stella faltered, the drift of these questions slowly dawning on her. She was amazed. It seemed incredible that he could take such a naïve idea seriously. Then she saw at once that he had noted her reaction, was intently following the expression of her face. She bit her lips; she was a fool. She was dealing with a professional.

'She was what, Miss Rushton?'

'She was simply friendly, like the rest.'

He referred to another of his devilish sheets. 'She says herself that she found him "quite a dear".'

'She is an actress. It's the way she talks.'

'That was not the impression she gave me.'

'She may . . . it is possible she tried to flirt with him.'

'You saw her doing that?'

'I . . . I noticed her trying.'

'And Mr Simpson, would he have noticed it?'

'He may have done. But it was nothing serious.'

'I see . . . nothing serious.'

The inspector pondered, as though what she had told him was highly significant. His manner of taking it made her wonder if after all it possessed some relevance. She experienced a depressing sense of inadequacy, of being unable really to judge the matter: it was something that required a trained mind, where the lay intelligence didn't count . . .

'Just one more question before I ask you to describe the events of Tuesday. It has to do with Mr Lea-Stephens' attitude towards your – friendliness – with his nephew.' The inspector paused, then added sneeringly: 'He discouraged it, didn't he?'

'No – on the contrary!' The denial was out before she could stop it. Only then, with her heart pounding, did she realise that she had been trapped. She stared wide-eyed at her tormentor, who stared back at her indifferently.

'Very well then, Miss Rushton. Now we will get on to Tuesday.'

She had to be prompted. She was shaken by the easy way he had manoeuvred her, the more so because it was done so perfunctorily and as though her attempted concealments were of no moment to him. She was humiliated, she felt helpless. She realised now how unprepared she was. The inspector was perhaps but an average detective but he was using a method that surprised and defeated her.

'So you joined the yacht at about half past eleven?'

'Yes . . . about then. It was nearly eleven when I set out . . . I stopped to talk to someone I knew.'

'Who was that?'

'George. He's an angler on a houseboat.' Why did her interrogators exchange glances when she mentioned that name?

'He would be a friend of yours, would he?'

'Yes . . . no, he's just an acquaintance.'

'How much of an acquaintance?'

'Does it matter? He lends me books.'

'What is his name, Miss Rushton?'

'I don't know. He's just George.'

They exchanged further looks; the inspector shrugged, then nodded. Again she had the bewildering expression that what she had uttered was unexpectedly significant. Did they know something about George? Was it damning to be his acquaintance? Both were looking at her with calculation, the younger man no longer bored. She felt her nausea returning. God, what had she got mixed up in?

'Who was on board the yacht when you joined it?'

'Simon . . . all of them except Woody.'

'And where was he?'

'I don't know. He was out in the launch.'

'Where was Keith Lea-Stephens?'

'He was there. He took in sail for me. Then he came and sat with us . . . we were all sitting under the awning.'

'Can you remember the conversation?'

She pummelled her brain for some vestige of it. As far as she could recall it had no bearing on what happened to Keith. 'We talked about the racing . . . about the yachts that were taking part. Then Simon suggested that we enter *Lutestring* in a race.'

'That who should enter it?'

'Keith and myself.'

'And did you?'

'No. I hadn't done any racing.'

'But you went out in it later, didn't you?'

'Yes. I was coming to that. I thought I would go for a spin in the dinghy, then Simon . . . he wanted to take photographs of *Lutestring*.'

'I would like to get that clear. You were going for a sail in your dinghy. You invited Keith Lea-Stephens to go with you, did you?'

'No! I was going on my own.'

'And then Mr Lea-Stephens made a counter suggestion?'

'Yes. He asked me to take *Lutestring* so that he could get photographs of her sailing.'

'And you invited Keith Lea-Stephens to go with you?'

'No . . . that is, I needed someone to crew me.'

'And Keith Lea-Stephens offered himself?'

'Well . . . yes, he was willing.'

'In fact, his uncle suggested it?'

'I couldn't take *Lutestring* without a crew.'

'I see. Now about the photographs. They were taken at long-range, were they?'

'They were . . . some of them were . . .'

'You mean there were others taken at closer range?'

'Yes. I came in close for some of them.'

'Mr Lea-Stephens requested that?'

'Yes . . . he was leaning over the rail, taking shots from above . . .'

By now she had given up trying to follow the aim of the questions. Her surrender of her own judgement as to what was relevant was complete. She had a dull sensation that she was playing a part in a drama of which she was ignorant, that all she had observed and surmised was ludicrously wrong and off the mark. She sat with her head slightly drooping. She felt beaten and worthless.

'What happened after Mr Lea-Stephens had finished taking the photographs?'

'We went sailing . . . about the Broad. Up the channel towards Alderford.'

'You moored, didn't you?'

'Yes, we moored . . . at a staithe with a boathouse. Then we went to look at a yacht. An old yacht, in the boathouse . . .'

'On the north side of the channel?'

'On the right-hand side. Going up.'

'That would be Tanner's Moorings.' He paused to glance at

another of the sheets. 'Did you see anyone there? Any boat that you knew?'

'I saw Simon in the launch . . . you must have it in his statement.'

'I would rather you answered my questions, Miss Rushton. Did you form an opinion as to what he was doing?'

'I . . . no. He was just out having a spin in the launch.'

'He wasn't spying on you?'

'I didn't say that!'

'He ignored you completely?'

'No, but I wouldn't say . . .'

'Then you saw someone else, did you?'

She nodded her head stupidly. 'Sam Fulcher. The man who wanted to be my gardener . . .'

'And what was he doing?'

'Just rowing. Watching us.'

'You seem to have been the object of a great deal of attention, don't you think?'

It went on and on. She had never guessed what it would be like. The sheer repetition of the questions wore down every secondary emotion. They wanted to be told everything though they seemed to know it all beforehand, and in the end it appeared futile even to imagine concealing anything. Yet she did. She managed to preserve those intimate facts about herself and Keith. By no trap or forced admission did they succeed in drawing these from her. They insinuated in a dozen ways that he was much more than her friend, but she found the strength to lie, however little they might believe her. And finally (it seemed after hours, though in fact it was barely an hour) they dismissed her with a suspended sentence:

'We would prefer you to hold yourself available, Miss Rushton.'

She left the room feeling drained completely, scarcely understanding where she was. She heard a question murmured in Simon's voice and shook her head. But she had only guessed what he had asked her.

27

She had her lunch blessedly alone. The others had already finished, and Simon had been called away to receive some instructions about the inquest. She ate mechanically, not noticing, her eyes fixed on the plate, her mind dazed and crushed and unable to think connectedly. So this was what it was like to be questioned by the police. To be reduced from an intelligent person to the status of an idiot. To be shown that one's mind was not sacred and impregnable, but unless armed, wholly vulnerable to the common shrewdness of a trained interrogator. The image of the inspector's casualness continued to float before her eyes. He had experienced no triumph, no complacency in trapping her. It was simply part of a routine that had been tried and proved effective, cold, scientific, a ready tool to dissect the mind. And how could one be armed against it? What was the formula of defence? At the moment this seemed more important than the death of Keith or anything else. What the inspector had got out of her was trivial but not the way in which he had done it, and she could see that it opened a door to the subjugation of human intelligence. Unless there was a defence, the mind's integrity was jeopardised.

But slowly these considerations faded before the more urgent facts of her situation. As she drank her coffee and smoked she began to shape her ideas more clearly. From the interrogation it was plain that the police were thinking as she had thought: that it was Simon who stood to gain and who might have engineered Keith's death. Did they know the full facts of Simon's relation with his father? Did they know as much as she, or were they better informed? There was one motive alone that stood up to scrutiny: this was what had emerged from the confused welter of facts. If Simon's second row with his father had been sufficiently serious, then the size of the stake involved might well have tempted him to crime. And did the police know of that second quarrel? Would they be informed of it by Simon's father?

The more she thought about it the more her uncertainty grew intolerable. One way or another, she needed to know in what horror she had become entangled. It might yet be an innocent tragedy and the appearances illusive, but if it were not then she needed the truth: she wanted to face it for what it was. And the kernel of the matter lay in the quarrel, of this she was convinced: she must fathom the importance of that if she were to decide on Simon's culpability.

By the time the coffee cup was empty she had roused herself from her stupor. A definite line of inquiry had begun to shape in her mind. She must know more of Simon's father before she could assess the significance of the quarrel. She marshalled together all she had heard of him. The picture that emerged was unfortunately hazy. He was stern, but not inhuman; he had rigid ideas, yet was polite and agreeable. He could inspire affection in Keith while being willing to sacrifice him to a selfish wish. He disliked actresses and promiscuity, yet could patch up a quarrel with a son on that score. He had built one of the major engineering firms and was absorbed by an ambition of continuing it in the family. This was all, as far as she could remember, and it was not enough for her purpose. The question in effect was one of intensity: was Simon's father inflexible enough to disinherit Simon?

She reviewed the sources for the possible augmenting of her knowledge: apart from Simon himself, there was only Dawn and Woody who had met the father. Jill too would doubtless have met him and would perhaps know as much about him as most, but Stella couldn't see herself going to Simon's secretary for information. Dawn's two-pennorth she already had, and Woody would be quick to smell a rat: he would simply clam up, and probably drop a hint to Simon. No: for information she would have to go outside Lazy Waters. An alternative source or two still remained for her to try. The head of Lea-Stephens

Engineering would scarcely have escaped notice in books of reference, while there was a columnist she knew: and there was always Jenny. Jenny, Stella remembered thoughtfully, had seemed to know a good deal about Simon.

She looked up: Simon was standing in the doorway, watching her. His face had been empty but now it broke into a weak smile. By a considerable effort she dissembled the revulsion she felt for him. She stubbed her cigarette energetically and rose from the table. He came into the room.

'They have fixed the inquest for tomorrow at ten.'

'Oh. Shall I be wanted?'

'No, my dear. Only self and Jill.' Then, noting her surprised look, he added petulantly: 'Only evidence of identification. They're keeping up this bloody farce.'

'I'm sorry.'

He made a gesture. 'I'm the one to be sorry. I feel an absolute swine, getting you into this pickle. I'm a bastard Stella, you'd do better not to know me. They gave you hell in there, didn't they? You came out white as paper.'

'I can't see how it was your fault.'

He gave her a long, pregnant look. Oh God, she thought, he can read my mind too. Then he turned away with a sigh, took a step towards the window.

'You don't know me,' he said slowly. 'I really am a bastard, Stella.'

She held her breath for a second, not daring to make a reply. It was too much like a confession and she found it throwing her into a panic. What should she do? What would be her position if he confessed? She wanted to know, but she realised fearfully that there could be danger in the knowledge. She said quickly:

'I want . . . I am going to Norwich this afternoon.'

He shrugged and faced her ruefully. 'Right my dear . . . you had better take the Metro.'

'Thank you, but the bus will do Simon.'

'Nonsense. You don't know our bus service. It's sketchy and sometimes missing, and it's misery to shop without a car.'

She let it go at that and accepted the key from him. He went with her down to the garage and opened the door for her. The Metro was an HLS with its own row of badges, and she did her best to reverse it out smoothly and with a respect proper to Simon's possessions.

'You will be back for tea, my dear?'

She nodded vaguely and closed her window. She could feel his eyes still fixed on the car as she drove it through the gates and on to the marsh road. Then she found she was breathing hard and was gripping the wheel like a learner driver.

28

Stella was unfamiliar with Norwich, its one-way streets and medieval eccentricities, and her patience was a little tested before she located the Central Library. This was a curious building that suggested an unfinished factory, an uneasy neighbour of the city hall and the large church of St Peter Mancroft. Stella parked and went in; signs directed her to the reference wing. Here, from low shelves stocked with bright, fresh volumes, she selected the current *Who's Who* and *Directory of Directors*.

In the former there were entries both for Simon and his father, Simon's paragraph being brief and extending only to six lines. His father had made more of an impression; his entry occupied half a column. Stella took it to a table where she could study it at leisure.

He was Arthur Seymour Kincaid Lea-Stephens, KCB, DSO, the only son of a Yorkshire family, educated at York, Greshams and Peterhouse. He had residences in the West Riding, Mayfair and Juan les Pins, and had married a Juliet Denbigh by whom he had issue. During the Second World War he had served in a Guards regiment, with distinction. He had endowed a laboratory for metallurgical research. He was chairman of Lea-Stephens Engineering and its subsidiary companies and among his recreations were listed shooting, yachting and racing. All this, or something like it, she had been expecting to find, and it merely corroborated her impression that there were Lea-Stephens millions; but there was one brief entry which she hadn't anticipated, a deadly little message contained in nine words in small italics:

President (founder member) of the League of Moral Reform.

She read it with a sinking sensation. It was the answer to her question. It put before her, as nothing else could have done, the man who was Simon's father. He was not disapproving, merely. His objection to Simon's behaviour was not passive. He was a militant, a reformer, and perhaps a moral fanatic; he might have forgiven Simon once, but the second occasion would find him adamant. She no longer had any doubt that Simon had been rejected in favour of the grandson.

She closed the book, leaving it on the table as the notices directed. Now it was done and she was certain she felt a dragging emptiness inside her. She went out into the street with its traffic, noise and sunshine, got back into the Metro and sat staring at the dashboard. But it wasn't the dashboard she could see. It was the dark and ugly mess. It was Simon, and the rest of them, and in the last instance herself. Because she was guilty too, however ignorant she had been: a pawn, but a pawn who had been all too willing. And Keith, in his innocence, had walked into the net spread for him, he had grasped at the pawn and become the inevitable victim . . .

Her hands tightened on the wheel. No – she wanted yet more proof! Still it was not enough to carry such a weight of horror. Before she could believe she needed every scrap of evidence, a foundation of circumstance from which dissent would be impossible. She climbed out of the car again and enquired her way to a phone box; there she scattered change on the top of the box, flattened her address-book, and dialled.

'Connect me with Lena Stott.'

She was kept waiting for several minutes; but at last the board at the Press Building got her through to the gossip desk. As the phone was snatched up she could hear the clatter of typewriters, and could visualise to herself the mayhem on the floor where Lena worked.

'Lena?'

'Why . . . Stella Rushton! Where have you been hiding away?'

She closed her eyes, trying to be patient under the barrage of questions and commiseration. It seemed so old, so far away, that childish business with Justin – how had it ever seemed important or likely to affect her foolish life? Finally Lena took the phone number and called Stella back so they could continue their conversation uninterrupted by the all-too-frequent pips.

'What do I know about Arthur Lea-Stephens? We know everything at The Press. Well, to kick off with, he's in line for a peerage.'

'Have you actually met him, Lena?'

'Bless your heart, of course I have. And Cliff Richards too. And the Reverend Ian Paisley.'

'What sort of a man is he?'

'Not your type I would have thought. He's pushing seventy anyway, though it's a well-supported case of seventy. But what gives, lover? Why this great interest in captains of industry?'

'Lena, I can't explain. It's just vital that I know about him.'

'Official secret, huh?' She heard Lena's throaty chuckle. 'Never mind, pet, I won't dig if it's sensitive. Well, he's tall, grey and handsome, he's the last of the sharp dressers, he's polite, he's condescending, and between ourselves a bit of a nutter. He gives a lot of bread away, mostly to undeserving causes, believes Mary Whitehouse is Saint Joan and Aunty Beeb the voice of the devil. When he talks of the evils of prostitution there's an unhealthy gleam in his eye, and the going gets even rougher when he's slating public immorality. Am I answering your question?'

'Yes.' Stella leaned against the wall of the phone box. Better than she knew Lena was filling in the detail.

'Want to know some more?'

'Yes . . . has there ever been any scandal?'

'There better hadn't be, not with a snow-white character like Lea-Stephens. But wait a moment – I'm forgetting his offspring. Would that be where the wind lies?'

'Simon.'

'Aha. Now I'm beginning to see the light.'

Lena chuckled again and it was easy to guess what she was thinking; but Stella felt too extinguished to expostulate with her. She let Lena revel in her imagined penetration. Later on she would know well enough what this call had been about . . .

'I've news for you, pet . . . or did you already have suspicions? If you know Simon then you'll know also that he's a Grade A womaniser. And you can do simple addition as well as the next, Stella. Am I right?'

'Just tell me, Lena.'

'Well, there's this whisper on the grapevine. It says that Simon's standing with his father isn't good. And it goes on to mention changes in a certain valuable document.'

'You mean a will?'

'So they say. On account of one actress too many. Have you met her, by the way?'

'Oh yes. I've met her.'

'Better watch your step, my poppet. There may be some angles you haven't spotted.'

Stella pushed closer to the comfortless framework of the box. 'This rumour,' she said. 'How much . . . how reliable is it?'

'Quote it at seventy-five per cent, which is high as they go. Another five per cent and I'd risk it in the column.'

'Does it say any more . . . about who is going to inherit?'

'It sure does. There's a grandson. You wouldn't be vamping him, would you?'

'Thanks, Lena.'

'You're welcome. Just invite me to the wedding is all.'

She rang off and without pausing dialled the number of Jenny's office. Again there was a wait, with typewriter-clicking in the background. She kept her eyes on the framed instructions screwed to the back of the box, striving to make her mind a blank. Only a seventy-five per cent rumour . . .

'This is Miss Williams.'

'Jenny. Stella.'

Followed another period of irrelevant exchanges. Jenny's solicitude was switched on like one of Simon's frank smiles, and Stella could do nothing about it but wait till it wore itself out.

'Jenny, I want to know something. Something about Simon and his father.'

'Oh dear, now! You are getting on with Simon, aren't you?'

'It's something else Jenny, and it's terribly important.'

'You know, you sound upset. You shouldn't be upsetting yourself.'

'Jenny, what do you know about them?'

At the other end there was a pause. She could imagine too well the obstinate expression that was slowly growing on Jenny's face.

'I don't think I ought to say, Stella. It is confidential, you understand. I may hear a thing or two now and then, but I never breathe a word outside the office.'

'But this isn't idle curiosity!'

'No, I can hear it isn't. And that is why I am being careful – I don't want anything foolish to happen. Now just what did you want to know?'

'He had a row – a row with his father.'

'Well, one does have rows now and then. There is nothing peculiar in having rows.'

'Jenny, this one was much more serious. It happened at Easter and concerned a woman Simon lives with. Her name is Davis, Glynda Davis. She had a part in one of his plays.'

'Oh. I might have heard about that.'

'Did he speak to you about it?'

'I won't say he didn't.'

'Jenny, for heaven's sake tell me what he said! I can't explain why, but it's too important to split hairs over.'

'Just a moment, if you please.'

Jenny's phone was laid down, and against the echoing background noise Stella thought she could hear a door close. Then the phone was picked up again.

'Now, Stella, listen to me. I am going to tell you what you are asking, though it is against my better judgement. But first I am going to warn you. You are a foolish woman, Stella. You can't help it, but you are, so I warn you to be on your guard. Don't go judging people hastily – do you understand what I am saying?'

'I understand, but it's too late, Jenny.'

'No, it isn't too late at all! And if it is Simon who is the trouble, let me tell you this about him. He is a liar, and a whoremonger, and he has no strength of character. I know these things because he was sweet on me, too. But a person can be like that and still be decent underneath it, and you will make a grave mistake if you think otherwise of Simon. You have failings yourself, Stella, but you are still a decent person.'

'But Jenny –'

'Very well, then. I have given you my warning. Now I will tell you what happened on the Wednesday after Easter. Simon was in here with some proofs – his flat is close to the office – and he sat down on the chair here, looking sick as a parrot. "What is the matter?" I asked him. "You are not yourself, Simon." "Nor would you be either," he said, "if you had just lost several million quid." I knew then what it was about, because he had had these rows before – there was one of them last summer that took a bit of living down. "Get along with you, Simon," I said. "The old man will soon come round." But he just shook his head. "No," he said, "not this time, my dear." Then he told me all about it. His father had got a promise out of him. It was after last summer, and he had promised to stay away from the women. And of course, he hadn't done it, and his father had put a spy on him – imagine that, will you! He had a private detective watching his son. So there it was, a complete bust-up, and all over a tart like Glynda Davis. The money was going to a brother's son and Simon would scarcely touch a penny.'

Stella had to press even harder against the wall of the box to prevent herself from sliding down it. She had it now in so many words, no longer a suspicion or a rumour. The police had only to hear this – as eventually they must – and there would be little use in telling them that Simon was 'decent underneath'!

'Stella, are you there?'

She choked. 'Yes . . . I'm here, Jenny.'

'Is that what you wanted to know?'

'Yes.' God forgive her that lie!

'Now remember what I told you – and also that this is in confidence. If he didn't tell me not to spread it around, that was because he trusted me not to. So keep it to yourself, Stella.'

'Yes. Yes, I'll do that.'

'And if you won't tell me what the trouble is, well never mind, but hold your chin up. It was going to kill you the last time but you are still here to tell the tale.'

She let the door slam behind her and walked shakily back to the car. She couldn't have been looking where she was going because on the way she bumped into several people. She started the car and began to drive, having no idea what the next step would be. She was a pawn. It was no use resisting the current of play which she couldn't control.

29

Stella couldn't bring herself to face Simon. She drove the Metro as far as the marsh track, just out of sight of the house, slipped the keys into the locker and very quietly closed the car door. It was teatime; a drowsy peace seemed to have settled over Iriston. She met nobody in the village or on her walk back to the cottage. So calm was the afternoon that it gave her a feeling of unreality, as though even its peace and assurance must hide an undiscovered threat. Pigeons were murmuring in the plantation, the grasses stood tall and unstirred by breeze, and her cottage, as she approached it, had the timeless appearance of a picture. Yet the threat existed: her intuition was sound. As she neared her gate, Fulcher rose from a seat in the hedgebank.

'I've been waiting for you, my girl . . .'

From the depths of her loathing she summoned the look she gave him. It didn't touch him. He merely grinned, his dark eyes switching about her hungrily. Then he put his foot against the gate to prevent her from opening it.

'Take your foot away from there!'

Her efforts to force it open seemed to amuse him. He kept grinning and parrying her attempts with a prodding toe.

'I'm going to complain about you. I'm going to complain to the police.'

'Oh are you, my girl? But I don't think you are, though.'

'And what's going to stop me?'

He edged a bit closer. 'I'll tell you if you don't know . . . and I reckon as how you'd better listen. I was out on the Broad babbing when your fancy man was done in. And I saw what I saw, and I don't know that I shan't talk about it.'

'You saw . . . what?'

'Never you mind. But the police'd like to know it. And where he went to and who was waiting for him – and who was watching for him when he came back. They'd like to know that, wouldn't they? Course nobody else haven't told them. And they aren't likely to find out while I keep my mouth shut.'

She pulled back from him involuntarily, her hand falling from the gate. So the brute knew it all – he had been there, an eye-witness! And now he was come to blackmail her for withholding information, and that after treacherously attempting to ensure that she did withhold it . . . She shrank back yet further. Was there no end to this nightmare?

'How much do you want?'

For answer he thrust his hand into his pocket. It came out with an untidy bundle of five-pound notes. He waved it under her nose, his grin fixed and malignant, then carelessly stowed it away again and leaned back against the gate.

'I don't want no money – not with Mr Simon around. I'm a valuable man to him right now, and he knows it. But there's other things besides money – that's right now, isn't it? What money won't buy, or that's what they say.'

'And you think that I –!'

'I don't have to think nothing.' He stuck his head out belligerently, his black eyes glittering. 'You might have kidded me before with your fancy parts and going-on, but you soon had a bloke hanging his hat here, didn't you? And what you can do for one you can do for another. You like it all right. I've seen, and I know.'

'You filthy beast.'

'Ah yes, you've got a tongue.'

'You can tell the police what you like.'

'That's likely, isn't it? But you're all right, my girl, that won't cost you a penny. I've taken a great fancy to you, and I'm a man what likes his fancy.'

He made a movement towards her, his hands reaching out, and suddenly she struck him a blow with all the force at her command. It was a swinging slap to the face which rang out like a shot: it caught him off-balance and tumbled him on to the road. She fled. She had the key out of her bag in a flash, darted in through the door of the cottage and slammed it shut behind her. She shot the bolts and leaned against it. She didn't know if he had followed her. She was shaking like a reed and laughing hysterically.

And it was then that she snatched at the idea that the cottage was a fortress, and that from now until the end she must remain in its protection. It represented her only defence from the evil about her: outside it she was vulnerable both to that beast and his master. She was dangerous, she knew too much. And she had put herself outside the law. Until Simon was taken into custody her safety lay in those four walls, and if she left them it must be in flight, to hide herself a long way from him.

She remained leaning against the door for some time, listening to the sounds from without, but at last she convinced herself that Fulcher had gone. She went cautiously to the window. Yes, he wasn't in the garden; and the gate which she had dragged shut was still closed, and the road deserted. Would he go to the police? Perhaps that was best, it would get it over. But she realised that this was unlikely unless he did it in a fit of anger. He had Simon on a string also and he wouldn't want to spoil that – in the long run, fivers were more acceptable to him than being revenged on Stella.

She began to calm down again as she moved about her small sanctuary. She filled the kettle and made some tea and drank cup after cup of it. Things were not so completely desperate. She had only to prevent herself from panicking. Simon could scarcely guess at the information that she had obtained that afternoon. For one thing, he was unaware that she had heard of the critical quarrel. It was Keith who had mentioned it to her, with a hint of what it had been about. She had been foolish, perhaps, to borrow the car and not to return it to the garage, but he could deduce nothing positive or damning from that. No, she wasn't in any danger as long as events moved quickly. If they were delayed . . . but she didn't want to think about that. The police would surely find Simon's father, they would learn what she had learned, and then it would be all over. It couldn't be long delayed.

She scraped a meal together and ate it sitting where she could keep an eye on the gate. If Simon came she was going to hide, to pretend that she wasn't at home. Tomorrow there would be a little respite because he had to attend the inquest . . . they might even arrest him there, producing and confronting him with his father. They were far from fools, those two detectives, they wouldn't have been wasting their time; they had no doubt contacted the French authorities and perhaps had already been in touch with their man. And what was the first thing they would ask him? 'Are your relations with your son cordial, Mr Lea-Stephens?' Then the cat would be out of the bag and they would pull in Simon to 'assist them' . . .

It grew dusk. Still she sat, revolving the thoughts through her brain. The doors were locked, the windows bolted and no light betrayed her presence. All the time she had been watching the gate but now she could scarcely make it out, and she could count on the fingers of one hand the vehicles that had passed by. Once a dog had come sniffing up to it but there had been no sign of the dog's owner; and now, for an hour at least, nothing had gone by at all. Did she dare go to bed? It was a quarter past eleven. The only sound she could hear was the ticking of a carriage clock. She rose and went into the kitchen to prepare some malted milk; but then, as she stirred the beaker, the phone exploded in a bomb of noise. Her heart thumped as she picked it up.

'Is that you, Stella? Simon here . . .'

She held the receiver away from her as though it might bite her, then dropped it back into its cradle.

She stood waiting; she knew he would ring again, and he did: three times. The last time he kept it going for at least two minutes. She thought it would drive her mad but she didn't dare lift it again. She stood rigid, her eyes closed, letting the sound jangle through her. Why was he so bloody, bloody insistent – what had he to say to her that was so imperative?

It ended, and she went back into the kitchen with her ears still ringing. The malted milk had got tepid and had a thick skin over it. She took it back into the lounge, sat mechanically and began to drink it. She knew now that she wasn't going to bed, not yet, not for a little while. He would come. She was certain of that. He wouldn't let the matter rest. He knew now that she was at home, though she had refused to answer his call. And there was the car she had left on the marsh track . . . now he would add that circumstance to the other. He would come. He would want to know what all this was about . . .

Through her whirlpool of racing ideas she heard a sound that drew a gasp from her: gently, and with great caution, the latch of the kitchen door was being lifted. Very slowly it rose, grinding faintly against the hasp, then, when it arrived at the top, came the creak of weight placed against the door. The creak was repeated once or twice before the latch was lowered again and, after a short but dreadful interval, the front door was given the same treatment. Stella was petrified. She sat motionless, even her lungs refusing to work. Her heart alone kept pumping away and driving the blood through her ears. No footstep accompanied the noises, there were no other sounds at all, and when they ceased nothing remained except the ticking of the clock.

Her lungs rebelled; she sucked in air in sobbing, hysterical gulps, broken occasionally by desperate pauses as she still strained her ears to listen. She put down the beaker. She felt about in the dark for a weapon. Her hand encountered the poker and she seized hold of it convulsively. It couldn't have been Simon, she had heard no sound of a car, and there hadn't been time enough for him to get down there on foot. Was it Fulcher? Had he returned to break in on her in the night? Or was it somebody else – some enemy unknown?

She had small time to think about it before a different sound reached her, and this time it was a car, its headlights glaring on the curtained windows. It stopped, its door slammed and steps hurried towards the cottage. Then the front door knocker rattled with half a dozen impatient strokes.

'Stella – are you there?'

It was Simon all right. Getting no reply he hammered again; he also rattled the latch.

'Stella, what's going on? I want to talk to you, Stella! You've been up to some fool game, and I'm damned well *going* to talk to you!'

She drew steadily back from the door, her teeth chattering, the poker raised. This was it, he had guessed what she knew. That damned car had given her away.

'Stella, I know you're in there!' The door groaned as he shouldered against it. 'Jenny Williams rang up. She admitted what she'd told you. Let me in, you blazing idiot – if you don't, I'll have this door down!'

A wave of panic swept over her: her actions became purely involuntary. She glided into the kitchen, unbolted the door, and slipped out. Then she ran, not caring if he heard her or not, she ran like an automaton in the direction of the summerhouse. But he did hear her, he came after her. He was shouting for her to stop. Only a score of yards behind her his feet were pounding down the path. She threw the poker into the trees and ran till she thought her ribs would burst, and she beat him, she got there first: she threw herself into the waiting dinghy.

'Stella listen to me, for Christ's sake –!'

She dragged at the knot and shoved herself off. A dark shape raced on to the staithe, dropped to its knees and made a grab for her. But she was away, rowing furiously. She was pulling away into the Broad. And he was left calling after her, a pleading, angry, impotent voice. She kept rowing. She didn't know, didn't care where she was going. She had escaped him this time and that was everything for the moment. The Broad was large and it was dark, she was safe from any attempt to find her. It had been deadly for Keith but it was a haven for Stella.

And then, with a terrific shock, she discovered that it wasn't safe at all: out of the darkness a second voice hailed her, the sneering, ugly tones of Fulcher. He was sitting perfectly still in his boat, letting her row up towards him, and now that she was only yards away he made his odious presence known.

'So you thought you'd come out to give me a treat like, did you?'

With a sob of terror she wrenched at the oars and sent the dinghy away on a different course. She heard his laugh and the dip of his oars as he took up the pursuit, skimming after her easily with long, lazy strokes.

'No, you won't get away like that, my lady . . .'

Pulling one stroke to her two, he was travelling faster than she was. The double-ender looked huge, its bows boiling through the water, and it was coming at her at an angle as though he meant to ram her. She twisted the dinghy round again but he anticipated the manoeuvre. He could turn his big boat with a single stab of the oar. In her desperation she was digging deep or missing the water altogether; it was too easy for him. She hadn't a chance of getting away from Fulcher.

'Can you swim, my girl? Like you can slap a man's face?'

Once more she made a turn, doubling like a pursued animal.

'That's a pity now, isn't it, wasting all that energy?'

She ground her teeth together. She pulled with the last ounce of her strength.

Then she saw that he was certainly preparing to ram her, and she knew that this time she would be unable to prevent it. The double-ender was surging towards her under all the power of his arms, his face showing as a pale splodge as he looked over his shoulder, judging it. She gave a cry. There was an impact, a sudden whirl and clamour of oars. She was thrown on her back into the fore-part of the dinghy. A hand grabbed her and she was heaved screaming on to some sort of platform, while behind her she heard Fulcher swearing and the thud and splash of frenzied strokes.

'All right . . . you can stop bawling.'

She tore herself free from the man who was holding her. Almost immediately something tripped her and sent her sprawling to the floor. A light was dimly shining on her through the open door of a boat's cabin. It was the cabin of the houseboat: and the man was George.

30

'*You'd* be the better for a drink, wouldn't you?'

George gravely stooped and helped her to her feet. He had such an air of matter-of-fact about him that her impulse to go on screaming died abruptly. But she stood trembling, and as far from the cabin door as she could. Her dazed mind was still struggling to comprehend this turn of events. Out in the darkness, growing ever fainter, sounded the splash of Fulcher's oars, then the silence of the night seemed to close in around them.

'M-my dinghy . . . what happened to it?'

'It drifted off, I'm afraid. But it won't go very far and I can fetch it for you later.'

'But I w-want it. Now!'

He shook his head decidedly. 'What you want is a drink first of all, and a moment to get over your scare. I'll fetch you a brandy. You had better sit down.'

She obeyed him uncertainly, her legs far from steady, and he vanished into the cabin, to return in a moment with two glasses. He handed her one. It contained three fingers of brandy.

'That better?'

She nodded, taking it down in gulps. George stood leaning against the doorway, sipping his drink evenly. He looked wretchedly solid, standing there, seeming to bludgeon her with reassurance, and yet . . . how did she know that she wasn't in a worse situation than ever?

'Perhaps,' he said, 'you had better tell me just what was going on out there.'

'It doesn't matter.'

'I'd say it does. He was all set to sink you.'

'He – he's got a grudge against me. I wouldn't let him do my garden.'

'Hmn. And what were you doing out here at this hour, in any case?'

A spark of rebellion snapped in her, doubtless assisted by the brandy. 'I don't have to tell you that! It's none of your business.'

He shrugged. 'You're in trouble, aren't you? There's a bit of undertow to this case. I would say that you know something and don't want to tell the police. And Fulcher comes into it somewhere. Is he trying to put the bite on you?'

She stared helplessly at the feet planted so firmly in the doorway. As usual he was on the mark, his instinct sure and undeceivable. Behind his comfortable practitioner's manner lurked the bright steel of the lancet and she was positive that he would use it with a firm hand and no pity.

'Suppose I am in trouble. You're a fine one to talk, aren't you?'

'Meaning what?'

'Meaning that the police have their eyes on you, too.'

He glanced at her speculatively. 'Naturally, they wanted a statement from me. I was here, on the spot.'

'Perhaps that's why they're so interested.'

He finished his drink and chose a seat on the far side of the well. There his face was in the shadow and she could see very little of him. 'I'll tell you something,' he said. 'Lea-Stephens was struck with an oar. It left the marks of rivets and copper sheathing. The police were checking on it this afternoon.'

'An oar . . . ?'

'Yes, an oar . . . like the ones in your dinghy. In fact, your dinghy seemed to interest them. They took plaster casts of your blades.'

A whirling sensation affected her head, she felt again the urge to begin screaming. Her voice was shrill as she faltered:

'But that's crazy . . . ridiculous!'

'The police don't seem to think so.'

'How could . . . it's fantastic! . . . why should I want to hurt Keith?'

'I believe they have got hold of the idea that you were revenging yourself on him.'

If she didn't scream it was only because she was on the verge of a faint, because the lamplight from the cabin was beginning to fuzz and sway about. It couldn't be, they couldn't think it: it was too wildly, naïvely impossible . . . it was like the idea they had had about Jeff Simpson — you only had to think, to consider a moment. And yet he had taken that seriously too, the icy inspector with his condemning eyes . . .

'You have to remember that they look at every aspect of a case.' George was talking again from the darkness he'd retired into. 'They collect the facts while trying not to jump to conclusions, then they fit them to this person, that, and the other. It isn't merely a question of seizing the obvious and proceeding with that. They try to get the whole picture before they move in a case.'

'But they can't – they can't believe such a ridiculous thing!'

'It isn't ridiculous, you know. It's a fairly shrewd choice. You had an opportunity which you made for yourself, and evidence of motive is public property. You had been cruelly jilted and you took your revenge on Lea-Stephens.'

'But I didn't – you can't believe it. You're a reasonable person!'

She could see his head shaking. 'I don't want to believe it, of course . . .'

'You can't, George, you can't! It's too ludicrously fantastic!'

157

'I'm sorry, Stella.'

'You can't!'

'You might have . . . well, people do have blackouts, don't they?'

She stared towards him wildly, feeling her reason slipping from her. Was it possible for him to believe it – a person apparently so sober-minded? But if he could believe it, what chance did she stand with the inspector? Could she herself believe in her innocence . . . had she done it, as he was suggesting?

'No!' she cried out. 'I didn't, I didn't, George. I never thought of such a thing . . . and on that night . . . I couldn't have! And the police don't know – they don't know what I know!'

'They know everything, Stella.'

'No – they don't know this!'

It came out. She couldn't stop herself. The words tumbled off her tongue. She had to kill that terrible doubt that she could hear in his voice. She spared herself nothing, she poured out the truth as she knew it. She told him everything about Keith, about Simon, about Fulcher. And he sat completely silent, listening, never interrupting her once. He let her talk and talk and talk until there was nothing more she had to tell him. A motionless figurehead, he sat listening in the shadows.

'But I'm not telling the police. They will find out, they must do. I couldn't bear it, George. I couldn't bear their questioning. I just want to be out of the way. I want them to get it over quickly. They don't need me, Simon's father can tell them . . .'

George stirred at last in his shadows. He rose massively to his feet; and then she was struck with a frightful uncertainty about what she had done. She had told him, but she had no idea what part he played in all this . . . had she once more, in her terror, stepped straight into a trap? He stood before her.

'So you are going to let the police figure it out, are you?'

She nodded mutely, her eyes wide, trying to read his expression.

'And suppose they don't?'

'But they will. As soon as they find Simon's father . . .'

'What makes you think that he would put his son in the dock on a murder charge?'

'He . . .' She stopped. 'But you don't want me to tell them, do you, George?'

He said nothing. He merely stood with his inscrutable face turned towards her.

'In fact, it isn't true that they think I did it. It's all a lie. You told me that to make me tell you what I knew.'

'It wasn't quite a lie . . . it was an idea the police considered.'

'And now you know . . .'

'Mmn.' He nodded. 'I think I have all the facts.'

'George, what are you going to do?'

'I'm going to advise you to amend your statement.'

'But I won't. I'm not going to tell the police!'

He smiled sadly at her. 'You've just told them.'

31

She didn't at once take his meaning, but when she did the colour rushed to her face. She sprang quickly from her chair and backed off behind it, her eyes fixed on his in anger and consternation. His smile still lingered. He made a placating little gesture.

'But I'm quite harmless, you know . . . and I might well have been a doctor. I've been told so by a man who is a good judge of character.'

'You – *you* are a policeman?'

'I have to admit it.'

'All the time – a policeman – watching, planted here!'

His smile grew broader. 'No, I haven't been planted here. We think we're competent, but we could hardly guess that a crime was going to be committed. I'm simply here on my holidays.'

'But you're one of them. One of *those*.'

'I'm sorry, I'm not even that. I'm only a stray from Central Office.'

She echoed his words: 'Central Office!' She knew well enough what they signified. The Central Office was what most people would think of as Scotland Yard. So he was more than a mere policeman, he was probably a name, one known to the media. Small wonder that the local inspector had shown interest in her acquaintance with George!

'And that's why . . . why you're incognito?'

'Because I'm a policeman?' He looked at her ruefully.

'Because – because you're known. Because your name would mean something.'

His shoulders moved. 'It's just a fad. I don't mind so much really. And anyway, there are plenty of people in these parts who know me.'

'Well, I don't. So perhaps you'd better tell me who you are.'

'Can't you think of me as George, and let it go at that?'

Stella shook her head. 'Tell me.'

'All right then – if I must! I'm George Gently, a Chief Super with a taste for the quiet life.'

'Then why did you pretend to be a doctor?'

'Well . . . that was your idea! And I thought I would play along, in case you didn't approve of policemen.'

'Why should you bother about that?'

'Even policemen have feelings, you know.'

Amongst the tangle of her emotions she felt a stupid prick of vanity and she paused, a little startled by this frivolous intrusion. She came out from behind the chair, where she had sought symbolic protection. She glanced at George questioningly, and then looked away.

'I'd love a fag if you've got one. I came away in rather a rush.'

'I'm sorry. I ought to have offered you one before.'

He went to rummage in the cabin, and this time she followed him. She was conscious of his browned, square-tipped fingers as he held her a light.

She smoked. He lit his pipe and added wreaths of smoke to hers. For a while he stayed silent, eyes fixed on a picture across the cabin. In a fresh bout of inconsequence she found herself comparing him to Sherlock Holmes, but if he did his thinking by pipes then this was evidently a one-pipe problem. When he came out of his abstraction he grinned at her and struck a fresh light.

'We'll let your dinghy drift. It's probably safe in a reed bed.'

'Then how do I get back?'

'The answer is that you're staying here. With one murderer and one minion out hunting your scalp you'll do best to stay put. I can offer you a choice of cabins.'

'And in the morning?'

'Then we'll go to Staybridge to amend your statement. I don't mind telling you that your testimony is going to clinch this case for them.'

Her terror returned. 'Oh God, I can never face Simon in court.'

'Give your imagination a rest, Stella. It's a sadly overworked faculty.'

He brewed them cocoa while she shamelessly smoked another of his cigarettes. She tried to go loose, to let the sudden panics drain out of her system. Then she found that she wanted to cry and she kept snivelling and rubbing her eyes, and all the time she was wondering about George: he still looked bewilderingly like a GP. How would she ever sleep again? How could she forget things for long enough?

He showed her to her cabin and lit the gas-lamp for her. When he had gone she didn't try not to cry any longer. She buried her face in a pillow and sobbed until she was exhausted, and at the end of her tears she must have fallen asleep.

George let her sleep late. She was grateful to him for that. At nine he woke her with a freshly made cup of tea. He had been out early, she learned, and had recaptured her dinghy; he had also rung the police at Staybridge and a car would collect them at eleven.

'I shall be taking your statement myself, if that's any comfort. I thought you would prefer it so I arranged it with Inspector Kirkham. I've also made other arrangements –' he shrugged an indifferent shoulder – 'things we conferred about yesterday. He and I are much of a mind.'

She sank her head. This would be his way of telling her of Simon's arrest. So she was safe again, free again, the time of terror was over. She wanted to ask him if Fulcher had been warned to stop persecuting her, but she felt unequal to talking about it and ate her breakfast in silence. That would be all straightened out . . . and anyway, would she be staying on here?

She washed their dishes and George dried them, his pipe in his mouth; and he too seemed preoccupied and unwilling to say much. She caught him watching her once or twice in his contemplative way, but he made no comment and only gave her a tiny smile. She had thought that Woody's face was unreadable but compared with George's it was an open book.

At ten to eleven they set out in George's dinghy, which sported a Seagull, he sitting at the helm and Stella perched in the bows. It was a short trip up the channel to one of the Broad's numerous landings, and waiting there as promised stood a shiny police Rover. With it waited the sergeant who had helped interrogate her yesterday; he came forward to take their line, but Stella cut him with great unction. As George was shutting-down his engine he and the sergeant held a muttered exchange, but of this Stella was able to gather only a few snatches.

'. . . got him first go . . . tried violence . . . the cuffs . . .'

'Did he ask . . . ?'

'Not yet . . . haven't charged . . . questioning . . .'

They were secretive, almost guilty about it, with their backs turned to Stella, and when the engine kicked to a stop they got into the car without more ado. Ten minutes later they were driving up Staybridge High Street, where it seemed that only moments before Stella had been wandering with Keith. They came to the police station and parked. The sergeant ran round to open the door for them. Stella noticed that he seemed to have a tremendous respect for George.

'In the waiting room, Chiefie . . .'

He led them into the building, past a desk manned by a

uniformed sergeant, up to a door in the hall. He gave George a nod. George said:

'If you will just wait in here, Stella . . .'

Obediently she entered the room, and heard the door close behind her. She looked about her. She stifled a cry. She was alone in the room with Simon.

32

He jumped up from his chair – not handcuffed, that was apparent, nor bearing any particular marks of violence on his person. He came towards her belligerently, his grey eyes flashing, and thrust his foot against the door which she was attempting to re-open.

'And a fine exhibition you've made of *yourself*!'

'Simon . . . don't touch me! I'm going to scream, Simon!'

'I'm not going to touch you, you flaming idiot.'

'I'll scream, Simon. I will!'

'Then scream your silly head off.'

She backed away, shuddering, leaving him in possession of the door. What had happened – what was going on? Why had they put her in with him like this? She threw a desperate glance at the window, but though it was open it had bars: she had no recourse but to scream, and to scream would precipitate his attack . . .

'For God's sake let me out Simon!'

'So that you can make a fool of yourself again?'

'I didn't know – I couldn't help it. I didn't know that George was a policeman.'

'Oh – so you blurted it out to him?'

'I tell you I was scared, and I didn't know!'

'You told him I was a murderer. You told him I murdered Keith for the money.'

'Simon, I couldn't help it.'

'What a pal. What a friend in need.'

She was back to the window now and pressing herself against the bars, but so far Simon hadn't moved, he continued to guard the only exit. He was staring at her with biting scorn.

'Well, you haven't hung me yet. And I've a feeling that you're never going to – what do you think of that, Miss Rushton?'

'It isn't going to help you, Simon –'

'Not strangling you, my favourite witness?'

'Your father – your father will tell them.'

'My dear, I shall settle *his* hash, of course.'

'Oh God Simon, you're mad!'

He gave a short, bitter laugh. 'You think so? From where I'm standing the case is different. But you're so loyal, aren't you, Stella? You're just the girl to stand by a man. You go poking around behind his back, then carry your dirt to the nearest policeman. As if there wasn't enough to bring them running, without your prying and hysterical nonsense.'

'It's too late, Simon. They know it all.'

'They do, my dear. But small thanks to you.'

'You can't do anything but plead guilty.'

'Oh thank you so much. I must tell my lawyer.'

He took some steps nearer to her, but keeping between her and the door. Then his anger faded suddenly, he looked older, tireder. He said wearily:

'Oh, hell! Do you suppose I couldn't guess what you were thinking? I could and I did. You gave it away a score of times. I nearly had it out with you yesterday after lunch, then . . . I don't know! It could be that I was too ashamed.'

She gulped tremulously. 'Ashamed . . . ?'

'Yes – that's what I said! Hasn't it occurred to your ingenious mind that I should be ashamed, my dear? You've done an awful lot of snooping and guessing and suspecting – isn't it a little ironical that you've missed the sordid truth?'

'But it's too obvious, Simon . . .'

He gave that bitter laugh again. 'It's obvious all right, and that's probably why you missed it. But I'm damned if I'm going to confess to you or anyone else – particularly to you, who are so prone to think the best of me. We're quits, Stella Rushton, we break about even. I'm a bit of a blackguard and you're a bit of a traitor. And we're both of us experts at explaining it away.'

'That's untrue – it's unfair!'

'Have I got to take all the blame?'

'I didn't trust you, Simon. And I never pretended I did.'

'You didn't have to trust me, but you might have drawn a line somewhere. It isn't funny when a familiar acquaintance tries to slip a noose round your neck. And as far as Keith went, you were willing enough there, Stella. You can't talk your way out of that – you needn't have grabbed him quite so readily.'

Her colour came. 'I didn't know . . . I didn't guess what it was about! And I needn't ever have met him. That was your doing, all of it. You had it schemed out from the start that I would be in a mood to respond to him. And Keith . . . you knew about that too, didn't you? That he had romantic ideas about me.'

'I didn't, as a matter of fact. But it was damnably convenient.'

'And you – you talk of shame!'

'I'm not ashamed of being successful.'

She stared at him unbelievingly, at his cool, assured complacence. She had heard that all murderers were mad, and Simon was scarcely sane at that moment.

'And you have no remorse at all?'

'Yes. It's illogical, but I have.'

'I suppose the logic is to blame your father?'

'No, that's the illogic. We're in the same boat.'

'I can't understand you, Simon.'

'My dear, that is too appallingly obvious. But you'll have to work it out as you go along, because dearest Simon isn't going to explain it. And now I think we've had enough of this farce. It's time we got down to the miserable business.'

He turned to the door, but as though on cue the door opened to reveal George. He stood smiling at them apologetically, and certainly they had heard no sound of his approach. He said mildly:

'I'm sorry to have kept you. Now, if you will just step into the office . . .'

He led the way. Stella followed Simon. She was completely at a loss. There was no sign of a guard on Simon, and the street door stood invitingly open. But Simon paid no heed to this, he seemed impatient to get to the office; he strode into it energetically and took a seat without being asked.

'We will deal with you first, Mr Lea-Stephens.'

The office was a cluttered and ill-lit room. Behind a desk sat the inspector and the sergeant, the latter looking more bored than ever. Stella found a chair at the side and George wedged himself in at the desk. Over all there was a smell of duplicating fluid, of floor polish and George's pipe.

'We will go over the details of what you were telling the inspector yesterday . . . I believe it is three years since you bought Lazy Waters?'

At Stella's elbow the WPC was scratching away with her pencil, a flesh-and-blood robot who came to life at the spoken word.

'You bought the cottage a little later?'

'In the March of the following year.'

'And you let it to a tenant?'

'I gave a friend of mine the use of it.'

'What was the friend's name?'

'She was Vanessa Lorraine. An actress.'

'Have you her present address?'

'No, but you can get it from her agent. A man called Abey Reynolds. You'll find him in the directory.'

'At what dates was she at the cottage?'

'If you mean last summer . . . from June till the middle of August.'

None of it was making sense as far as Stella was concerned, but she had given up expecting the police to make her kind of sense. Perhaps George was loosening Simon up, getting a steady flow of responses from him. George, she recalled, could go to the point fast enough when it suited him.

'Was there a daily woman at the cottage?'

'A Mrs Yaxley. I still employ her.'

'And Samuel Fulcher looked after the garden?'

'He was supposed to go twice a week.'

'He gave satisfaction?'

'That was the impression. Certainly Vanessa never complained.'

'Did she ever discuss him?'

'Let's say she made some remarks that were highly suggestive.'

'Touching her relations with him?'

'Yes. And he confirmed that in a recent conversation.'

George paused, and the flickering pencil came to an expectant halt. 'What are your personal impressions of Fulcher?' he asked.

Simon tapped his forehead. 'He isn't strong up there . . . paranoia is my diagnosis, but then, I'm only a layman. And of course he is over-sexed. But so was Vanessa.'

'You had a complaint about him from Miss Rushton?'

'Yes – and I spoke to him. On the morning of Regatta Day.'

'How did he take it?'

'You might describe him as being surly and abusive. He said he wasn't paid by me any longer and I knew what I could do.'

'Was that when he confirmed that he had been intimate with Miss Lorraine?'

For the first time Simon looked uncomfortable. 'That was in a subsequent conversation.'

'When was that, Mr Lea-Stephens?'

'It was after lunch yesterday.'

'What was the substance of the conversation?'

'He had come to discuss what had happened.'

George eased round in his chair to stare flatly at the wall. 'Fulcher had lately come into two hundred pounds in five-pound notes, Mr Lea-Stephens. Would I be correct in supposing that he obtained the money from you by threat . . . knowing, for instance, that you had lied to the police?'

'That isn't true!' A flush had appeared on Simon's face. Stella's heart thumped: now it was coming, the inevitable steel from under the cloak. George picked up the fatal sheets which were stacked ready on the desk. He turned them over casually, skimming the typewritten lines.

'On the morning after the tragedy you came down the Broad in your launch. You say that the time was at or about nine a.m. You saw Fulcher babbing for eels and you stopped to enquire of him about your nephew.'

'That is perfectly true!'

'But at nine a.m? Is that when one goes babbing for eels?'

'He – he was fishing then, or something!'

George shook his head cheerfully. 'He was babbing for eels all right, because he was hawking them in the village later. Now I put it to you that one a.m. is a more likely time for the pursuit?'

Simon glared at him, but he was caught, and Stella was holding her breath. For a few moments there was silence except for a murmur of voices from the direction of reception. Then George added, very quietly:

'I want to remind you of the importance of this. You must have gathered by now the direction of our enquiries.'

'Oh, hell!' Simon threw out his hands in a pettish gesture. 'You are going to have it, aren't you? You won't be happy till you do!'

George was staring at the wall again. 'The details don't concern us, Mr Lea-Stephens. You would naturally be a little anxious about these moonlight swims of your nephew.'

'All right then – it was just that!'

'You were out looking for him?'

'Yes.'

'And at about one a.m. you met Fulcher, babbing for eels. So you enquired if he had seen your nephew, who was out on one of his swims. He hadn't, so you gave it up and returned to the yacht. Is that the substance of your testimony?'

'It's all you're getting out of me!'

'Thank you, Mr Lea-Stephens. That is really all we require.'

There was another and shorter pause, then Simon jerked to his feet.

'You have finished with me? I can go?'

'Yes . . . but please remain available to sign your statement.'

Simon dashed a look at Stella in which triumph and bitterness were mingled, then he went quickly through the door and closed it very hard after him. Nobody moved to prevent him. Now the inspector, too, was looking bored. Only George, in his pacific way, seemed to be enjoying the proceedings. He gave Stella a little twinkle.

'Now it is your turn, Miss Rushton.'

She caught her breath snatchingly. 'But Simon . . . aren't you going to . . . ?'

'Simon?' George looked surprised. 'You heard his statement. It places Fulcher at the scene of the tragedy, which was the testimony we needed.'

'*Fulcher?*'

'Yes, Fulcher. I thought perhaps Lea-Stephens would have explained to you. Fulcher is under arrest and we are about to charge him, but naturally we want your amended statement first.'

Somehow she got through it, with generous prompts from George. Her bewilderment, almost angry, was pushing her to the edge of tears again. She didn't believe it, George had sprung it from nowhere, it didn't square with her aching ideas. It had to be another one of those police fancies, so strangely wide of her intuitive certainty . . . And yet all George was getting from her had to do with Fulcher; he was ignoring her detective work, her proof positive against Simon. Could this be the truth at last, so dully commonplace and undramatic? Had she to shed her perfect interpretation and to accept this homespun, makeshift alternative?

'I think that covers it, for us.'

George had done all he could to let her off lightly. He had smoothed over facts, neglected to clarify, and simply turned his back on things that would have embarrassed her.

'We will get this typed . . . it will take about an hour. Then you can sign it, and that will be that, Miss Rushton. I may perhaps add that a trial seems unlikely. The doctor's impression is that Fulcher will be classed unfit to plead.'

It was anticlimax after anticlimax. She could but shake her head stupidly. No trial, no publicity, no hideous ordeal waiting ahead. It was as though George had pricked with a pin the tremendous fantasy she had created and now, deflated, it lay at her feet, mocking her with its absurdity. The truth was not dramatic at all. It was only surprising and wretchedly commonplace.

Still shaking her head she rose and made her way to the door. George followed her after a few parting words to his colleagues. It had the air of a breaking up after a show or a sporting fixture, the issue settled, nothing left but to go home. Outside in the street he pointed to a café and fell into step behind her. She went with him unresistingly. She was glad to be provided with an object.

'I'm sorry if it didn't quite come up to expectation.'

She smiled weakly at him, no longer surprised when he read her thoughts.

'You thought it would teach me a lesson, didn't you? Being shoved in there with Simon.'

'I thought you might straighten things out between you.'

'We did. We're on intimate terms of enmity.'

'You were both of you a bit to blame . . .'

'Oh, he told me that himself.'

'Let's grab ourselves some coffee. Then I will give you my version of it.'

33

The café was a conversion of two old cottages and they had no difficulty in finding a secluded corner. Coffee came in large, pastel-tinted cups and was accompanied by a plate of solid-looking pastries. George drank coffee and ate a cake before he said anything else, then he filled and lit his pipe, directing the puffs towards the ceiling.

'Well . . . you were right about one thing,' he said.

'Thanks. But don't flatter me too much.'

He smiled. 'There really was a lot of driving power in the Lea-Stephen millions. Our friend Simon is wealthy, but wealth is a comparative term. And Simon, as you may have noticed, is fond of spending the stuff as he gets it.'

'I'm glad to have your confirmation.'

'So far you read the situation correctly. But you were wrong in your deductions as they applied to Mr Simon.'

'It was sufficient motive, wasn't it?'

'Oh yes. Almost too much! But you should have made an allowance for character, and violence isn't obviously Simon's line. He is more civilised, more devious, the product of a steadily affluent culture. He was certainly after his father's money, but by methods that fell short of criminal.'

'Then all that pushing of Keith on to me . . .' Stella's cup clattered in her saucer. Why did it come like a revelation, what ought to have been plain from the beginning? 'And the spying – the photographs! They were all part of his plan?'

George shaped a small smoke ring. 'That's the way I see it. To be frank, you were his second string, an alternative to Miss Le Fay. Simon was out to seduce his nephew and Miss Le Fay was his original choice, but then you applied for the cottage and he realised that you would make a likely reserve. And his second string did the trick . . . I'm sorry, but isn't that how it worked out?'

She bowed her head over her plate. 'The kid was a lost soul,' she said. 'He needed help . . . he really did. But of course, it was selfish too.'

'Yes. It had to be, a little.'

'A lot. Oh, and I loathe Simon!'

'It isn't one-sided, don't forget. You did credit him with murdering his nephew.'

She wanted to tell him that this was different, that it arose from no baseness of her own, but she didn't: she accepted the reproof at his hands. He was right, after all. She should have known Simon better. And she did know him better, but she had chosen to set that knowledge aside. She had had reason, God knew; yet in a way she was still to blame. She saw that she had perversely wanted him guilty, a scapegoat for the guilt she had felt herself. It balanced out: she had very small grounds for a pose of righteousness.

'And Fulcher,' George went on. 'Well . . . we know a little about his background. He comes from a local family with a history of instability. He's something of a hermit. He lives on his own in a clay-lump cottage on the marsh. He's given a bit of trouble before . . . with women, you know. And occasional violence.'

She shivered, remembering the night before. 'Why have they never locked him up?'

'Oh, you have to give people their chance . . . they're all human under the skin.'

'But Keith . . .'

He gave his comfortable shrug. 'I doubt whether Fulcher meant to kill him. There was his successful rival swimming home, and Fulcher gave him a bang, just to go on with. A spiteful and jealous blow . . . but it chanced to render the young man unconscious.'

'Please, George! Don't go into that.'

'I am sure that's the way it happened.'

'I can't – I can't bear to think of it.'

'But you must have it out before you can forget it.'

Yes, she must have it out: she understood the truth of that. There must be a time to think it through, to collect the vision of it into a focus. But not now, not at that very moment. Her mind wasn't ready for it, yet.

'Someone told me I was a foolish woman . . . and that's true, George, isn't it?'

He chuckled, wrinkling his eyes. 'Do you mind much?' he countered.

'I'm not sure whether I mind. But I can't help being foolish. I just panic, and imagine things . . . and I'm a selfish woman, too.'

'It isn't without its charm, you know. When so much frankness goes with it.

'But I would rather not be foolish in the company of sensible people.'

'You'll do,' he said, signalling the waitress. 'You'll do on weekdays, if not on Sundays.'

It was too light-hearted, nearly flirtatious, and her treacherous tears were upon her again. She bit her lips and forced a smile. No hands, she thought. It had just occurred to her that she wasn't wearing a smudge of make-up.

34

Perhaps the worst of it all was that she could forget Keith so quickly, so that within a few days she had difficulty even in remembering what he had looked like. She was obliged to admit afresh that he had never been important to her, and that when the shock of his death had receded she was rather impatient at the thought of him. Keith had been forced upon her, but he had forced himself upon her too. She had never seriously accepted him except as a distraction. At first she had blamed herself for that but the blame was more romantic than real; his pursuit of her had been egoistic and had made no demands on her sincerity. They had been intimate but they had been strangers, each in search of his own end. His tragic death had given the affair a false significance but now that falseness was becoming plain. Someone, she felt, should be grief-stricken about Keith, but she knew that someone could not be her.

She made her peace with Simon; this called for a little magnanimity. George could draw up what balance he liked, but Stella knew what she knew. She let a couple of days pass because she had heard that Simon's father was down there, then one evening she lifted the phone and dialled the Lazy Waters number. Simon answered.

'Hullo Simon.'

'Oh, hullo.' He sounded weary.

'Is your father still with you?'

'No.' He sighed. 'He left this morning. The funeral is in Yorkshire. I'm running up there tomorrow. And I'm dead Stella, completely dead. The others have scuttled back to town.'

'Can you face up to seeing me?'

'Not if you're going to bawl me out.'

'I'm not going to do that, Simon.'

'You had better come then. It'll make a change.'

She took care not to arrive until after his usual hour for supper, and she found him drinking coffee in his favourite chair in the lounge. He was alone. The piano where Woody had played was shut, the settee was no longer draped with Dawn, no voluptuous Glynda cast jealous eyes. By itself, near the French windows, stood the chair on which Keith had sat reading her poems, and down the lawn, beyond the willows, the heedless boats passed. Simon rose when she entered, giving her a haggard, appealing look. Then he rang for some fresh coffee and threw himself down again.

'Should I make my apology now?'

She shook her head. 'I don't think so, Simon. I've had time to mull it over and it seems pointless to make apologies.'

'My father guessed what I had been up to.'

'I'm sorry. That couldn't have been fun.'

'It wasn't. And here's the strange thing. We patched it up over the coffin.'

'I'm truly glad of that, Simon.'

'I'm more surprised than anything else. I'm one of the undeserving rich – I fall on my feet every time.'

She didn't stay long, nor did Simon seem to expect it. The whole point of the visit was that she had made it. As she was leaving he took her hand and pressed it warmly, but that was all. They had returned to the footing of friends and the rest was best left unspoken.

It was not so easy to settle what her footing was with George and she had little time to explore the problem, since his holiday finished at the end of the week. She spent his last two afternoons with him, and learned a lot about angling. She also elicited that he was probably in love with his wife. He was friendly, but never offered a pass. He seemed to enjoy her company, as she did his. He liked her to talk, admired her she was sure, and they appeared to have many tastes in common; yet had she truly made an impression on George, would he want to see her again? For the answer to this interesting question she was kept waiting till the very last moment. Then, as she was about to depart from the houseboat, leaving him with bags packed for the morning, he went carelessly round his pockets in search of a card for her.

'We'll perhaps meet again when you're back in town. You are coming back, aren't you?'

She made up her mind instantly. 'Yes. I'll be back quite soon.'

'I work unsocial hours, you know, but I can usually sort something out. My wife is French, and besides the flat we have a house near the sea in Suffolk.'

She jotted her address on the leaf of a notebook and George inserted it carefully in his wallet. As she rowed off down to the summerhouse she felt a complacency that was delightful. The reeds were tall in their summer greenness, the heron guarded the water lily. Leander was dead, but it didn't matter. She was a foolish woman, but she was free.

Brundall, 1982

*If you have enjoyed this book
and would like to receive details
of other Walker Mystery titles, please write to:*

*Mystery Editor
Walker and Company
720 Fifth Avenue
New York, NY 10019*